Alpha's Arranged Marriage

Shifters of Clarion

Lila Bosch and Ariel Renner

Copyright © 2024 by Lila Bosch and Ariel Renner

www.arielrenner.com

All rights reserved.

No part of this publication may be reproduced, distributed, or transmitted in any form or by any means, including photocopying, recording, or other electronic or mechanical methods, without the prior written permission of the publisher, except as permitted by U.S. copyright law.

The story, all names, characters, and incidents portrayed in this production are fictitious. No identification with actual persons (living or deceased), places, buildings, and products is intended or should be inferred.

Contents

Chapter One – Thea	1
Chapter Two – Xander	9
Chapter Three – Thea	20
Chapter Four – Xander	31
Chapter Five – Thea	43
Chapter Six – Thea	56
Chapter Seven – Xander	72
Chapter Eight – Thea	87
Chapter Nine – Xander	102
Chapter Ten – Thea	113
Chapter Eleven – Xander	117

Chapter Twelve – Thea	126
Chapter Thirteen – Thea	137
Chapter Fourteen – Xander	146
Chapter Fifteen – Thea	158
Chapter Sixteen – Xander	167
Chapter Seventeen – Thea	177
Epilogue – Thea	190
Special Preview – Alpha's One-Night Stand	195
Free book from Ariel Renner	202
About the Author	203

Chapter One — Thea

"I am telling you, I almost lost it when the lady told me a second time that I got her order wrong when it was the exact order she placed," Ethan laughs as we make our way home.

It's ten at night, and the streets of our little neighborhood are now empty save for a couple of people who happened to pass us by about a block back—a man hurrying home and a woman jogging in the other direction. Our little town of Creek Falls opens at dawn and closes at dusk like most sleepy towns tend to do. It's a safe place. In fact, I'm pretty sure there's some national statistic on that somewhere. We have to be on some kind of list or something. The thing about safe towns, though, is that they also tend to be extremely boring. But it's my home. It's the only place I've ever lived. However, that has never stopped me from dreaming about a better life far away from here.

The major issue with small towns is that everybody's always in everybody else's business. I feel like a flea doesn't sneeze here without it making the ten o'clock news sometimes. It's hard to have any kind of social life when the whole town is watching you and gossiping in the shadows. I guess that's why Ethan is my only friend these days. He's not as nosy as everybody else around here.

We're laughing as we talk about the day we just lived through at the diner. Crazy customer stories are the one thing we share implicitly. I sigh and say, "Our day wouldn't be complete if customers didn't mix up their orders or forget what they ordered."

"Yeah," he chuckles. "That's what we get for working the night shift."

As work friends go, Ethan is the best. I think he might be the only thing that's been keeping me sane so far . . . and when I leave this Podunk town, he's the only person I'll miss. We've always covered each other's shifts when personal issues popped up, and we've always had each other's back. He's a good person. Truly.

I guess that's why I haven't spoken to him about my plans to leave this wretched town in two weeks. I'm pretty sure he'll tell me it's a bad idea.

"What will you do there?" he'd ask. I don't even know how I would respond to that. I mean, you'd think he'd understand. I just turned twenty-three. Most people my age are getting apartments in New York somewhere and living fast-paced lives, while I just languish in "Smalltown, USA." It's long past the time for me to leave this place once and for all.

The thing is, I don't have much planned out yet. I know I'll have to find a new job, and there's a community college that I can attend, *and* it just so happens to be near the apartment that I put down a deposit on . . . but that's as far as I've thought about it. I've saved up enough money so I can stand on my own feet for about six months, maybe even a year if I eat ramen every day. I'll manage. I'm sure of it. It's hard to tell somebody else that, though. If I tell Ethan I'm leaving now, he'll just talk me out of it and maybe try to tell me I should have a better plan before I uproot myself.

We reach Ethan's house. "Alright," I say with a smile. "I'll see you tomorrow."

"You sure you're good to walk the rest of the way?" he asks. We're standing right in front of his walkway, and I have to admit, I'm a little jealous that he's only got a few steps before he's home. "It's no big deal," he adds. "I mean, it's not that far of a walk back for me."

"You ask me that every night, and every night, I end up being fine." I nudge him on the shoulder a little. "We're in the safest city in the world, remember?"

"According to who?"

"I don't know. But nothing ever happens here, right? I'll be fine."

He looks at me skeptically. Then, just like he does every night, he caves in and says, "Okay. Good night, Thea."

As I make my way down to the next block, where my lonely little apartment is, the streets are quiet with nothing but the sounds of crickets as my company. I walk past several houses, their lights flickering off. In the darkness, I barely catch a glimpse of my reflection in the windows—short in stature, long platinum blonde hair tied back in a ponytail, curvy but barely big enough to convince anyone I'm eating well. Glancing into the darkened houses, I imagine families turning in for the night. Mom and Dad carrying their sleeping children to bed, a little brother draped over his father's shoulder. I envy them the peacefulness of the normal family's daily routine. I'm so far removed from that I can't even imagine a night that might end that way.

A chill in the air raises the hairs on the back of my neck, pulling me from my wistful thoughts. I don't know why, but it's as if something dark is looming above me. I slow my walk a little, glancing around carefully. There's nothing around me. I get to the corner right before the block where my apartment is, and my stomach tightens. Out of nowhere, the lights of a car glare out at me from the darkness. It's barreling down the road toward me, way over the posted speed limit. The sound of the engine cuts through the air, shaking the very concrete of the sidewalk like thunder in the quiet night.

For a split second, I think that they're going to speed past me. But the car crosses lanes, and the headlights beam straight at me. Panic sets in, and my feet start moving before I'm fully conscious of what's happening.

I'm running as fast as my feet can carry me, bolting back toward Ethan's house. The car hops the curb and swerves, barely missing me as I trip over my own feet to avoid it. I scramble up and sprint for the alley that I just walked past.

I keep running, turning down a bend behind a building and jumping over a fence to get to the alley on the other side of the next street. In that next alley, it occurs to me that I don't hear the car anymore. I stop and look around, panting to catch my breath. I've lost them . . . I think. I don't know.

The driver might've lost control of the car. Or maybe he was drunk. It's weird that I got it in my head that they were *trying* to hit me. It was probably an accident.

I lean against one of the buildings and rest my head against it, taking long, deep breaths. Maybe I should call the police. Maybe . . .

My stomach tightens again, and the hair on my arms stand up. I look around just in time to see a figure of a man standing in the dark alleyway.

I scream and stumble back, landing hard on my ass. I scramble to my feet as the figure takes two steps closer to me. I turn back around and nearly crash into two more men behind me.

The men, all dressed in black, have me trapped in the narrow alley, cutting off both avenues of escape. I open my mouth to scream, but one of the men grabs me and shoves a handkerchief in my face, covering my nose and mouth. The last thing that goes through my mind before it all goes dark is that I should have left this fucking town sooner.

My eyelids are heavy as I swim up from unconsciousness, a dim light invading my sight. My head is pounding, and my mouth is dry. The sounds of different voices surround me.

"She's awake," a strange voice says somewhere off to one side.

Instinctively, I try to turn my head, but I can't. I try to move, but I'm lying on something hard. It feels like a heavy weight is keeping me down. I can't move. The voices continue around me. They are speaking words that I don't know—it sounds like a song. No. Like a chant. Through the dim light, I'm starting to make out figures . . . shapes . . . Oh, no.

A ring of white-cloaked people looms over me.

I open my eyes and see the ropes tying my arms down. I'm bound to some kind of hard, flat surface, and suddenly, it all seems eerily familiar. I've dreamt of this many, many times before, but it's never felt this real. Am I dreaming? Oh, please tell me that I'm dreaming.

No, no, no, no, no, please. I shut my eyes. This is just the dream—that same damn dream I have over and over again. I just need to wake up. Oh, please, let me wake up.

My eyes sting with tears as the cloaked figures continue chanting, the words getting higher and faster. I'm so scared.

Then the chanting stops. I look around to see them part to one side. A larger, broad figure walks past them and toward me. An all-consuming fear takes over me as their chants start up again, getting faster and louder. A fervor overcomes them as the large man takes out a knife. My eyes grow wide as the long blade catches a sliver of light. He stands over me and holds it to my chest. In terror, my breath leaves me, and everything goes dark.

Chapter Two — Xander

We're sitting in the living room, my hands moving lazily up and down Rhiannon's bare legs as they drape across my lap. I was finally able to get out of the boring meeting that held me for the past three hours. I would rather be in bed with Rhiannon right now, but she wants us to just sit together and talk about little things, so here I am, settling for this kind of skin-to-skin contact.

"Training went well today," she says, "even though it wasn't the same without you around."

I train my eyes on hers, letting my view of her drift to her lips before moving all around her face. With her lovely auburn hair framing her face in large ringlets and her soft brown eyes against her alabaster skin, she is a beautiful woman. So much so that she is deceptively ruthless on the training ground. It's what first attracted me to her. Her edginess mixed with her softness.

"I wished I was there to watch you whoop their asses out there," I reply. She smiles at my words and leans in to kiss me.

"I hope I am not interrupting?" A quiet yet commanding voice breaks the moment.

We both look up, and in one swift move, Rhiannon's legs slide off mine as she stands. She adjusts her long dress, smoothing it out with her hands. Looking at her, a casual observer would think we were doing something wrong, but the mere presence of my mother usually elicits that kind of behavior from everyone. My brother and I are the only ones who don't have to stand upright whenever she walks into a room.

"No, of course not," Rhiannon says quickly. A smile curves across my lips at the sight of her on her feet.

My mother's face softens at her reaction. "It is okay, dear. I just need to speak with my son."

I stay put, observing them both, pondering if this is how they will interact after we officially become mated. I wonder what she will be like as the Luna to my Alpha.

Rhiannon gives her a short nod, then leaves the room. It's just my mother and me now, but I can hear the steady heartbeats of the seers just outside the door.

"How did your meeting go?" She walks all the way in and sits down on the chair to my left.

"Productive. We reinforced our relationship with the Tivaci Pack and have also sent aid to the injured in the Nodi Pack."

"Mm. It's very sad what happened to them. No one should have to go through such horrifying circumstances," she says.

The scary stories I have been told about the curse that has befallen us don't seem like stories anymore. They're now our reality. Every day, we live trying to find a way through the chaos, a way that would guarantee we make it out of this alive.

Every full moon since the curse's inception, it seems to get worse. Our little section of Clarion has had to be quartered off from the rest of the kingdom just to keep things contained, but I don't know how long that will last. The last full moon, rage and bloodlust were at their peak. The members of the two packs clashed in the streets, ripping each other apart while the Shamans just stood by and watched. It was a massacre among kin.

"I have spoken to our seers," Mother says. "They have just revealed to us information that is vital to the survival of this pack."

This immediately piques my attention. Whenever our seers receive messages, we never take them for granted. I sit up, expecting her to answer right away. She doesn't. She just regards me with hesitation in her eyes.

"Okay," I press. "What is it?"

"I wanted to do this myself because I understand that it's a delicate situation and shouldn't be delivered to you by just anyone."

She's circling the issue. "I'm listening."

She takes in a deep breath, then, "The seers, after enough confirmation, just told me that Rhiannon is not fated to be your Luna."

I hear her heartbeat skips a little, but it's otherwise as steady as a rock. I calmly stand up and walk around to the back of the couch, my claws hook into the padding.

"What do you mean?" I ask her in as calm a voice as I can.

"The Moon Comet is fast approaching. With the curse being what it is, we fear what will happen once it arrives. The seers have been working day and night for a solution, and it seems that they have found one. They've found her—the one who is fated to be your mate. She's the key to our survival, and you play a crucial role as the Alpha of our pack and this region."

I can't believe what I'm hearing. Rhiannon is the one I chose, the one I want to be mated with. Now, my mother tells me that can never be? I take a breath, working to calm my emotions. "What makes this . . . person so special that she will break the curse? Why must *I* be the one?"

"You are the Alpha, my son," she says gently. "And she is born of wolf and Shaman."

And now I understand. The only thing said to break the curse is a special being born of wolf and Shaman blood. I never believed such a creature could exist.

"You will need to be wedded before the Moon Comet's arrival," she says simply. "Once she is found and brought to us, we will make the necessary arrangements—"

I tear into the fabric of the couch with my claws, my anger overcoming my self-control. I rip through wood, fabric, and cushion as I roar with anger. This cannot be!

Mother just watches, her hands clasped together on her lap, her eyes calm and gentle. I try to take a breath, try to calm myself, but I'm enraged enough to let my wolf out.

"Let me get this straight," I growl. "Since our childhood, Rhiannon and I have been expecting to be mated, and now, all of a sudden, it's someone else? Just like that?"

My mother sits in her usual regal manner, still calm and offering me no reaction to my rage. "Not just anyone else." She stands and takes a step toward me. "The Chosen One, my dearest Xander. She will be the one to save every one of us from impending doom. You must join with her to spark her powers. It can be no one else."

"Rhiannon is the only woman I have ever loved!" My voice booms through the room and reverberates off the walls. "You cannot expect me to fall out of love with her only to fall in love with someone else?"

"This has nothing to do with love," she says in an even, precise tone. "This is about saving your region. Xander, no wolf has been able to leave or enter this portion of Clarion since its inception, and that has been carefully orchestrated to keep the curse from spreading . . . but one day it will."

"No," I say, shaking my head. "We have safeguards. The people are protected—"

"Nothing lasts forever. Eventually, this curse will spread and destroy everyone in Clarion. If we have some way to solve it now, we must take it. There is no other way."

I don't have anything to say. I'm caught between my duties and giving up the one constant of my life. Mother touches my arm lovingly and says, "I know that this is hard. If I could change any of it, I would. I swear it. But it must be done. Xander, you must do what an Alpha does for his pack and his region. You must protect us."

I rub my eyes and walk away from her to the other side of the room. The need to keep my body moving just to calm the animal inside me is overwhelming. I am incensed.

I have lived my life in service to my pack, and up until now, I believed that with Rhiannon by my side, the burden of being Alpha would be eased.

"I am so sorry about Rhiannon," Mother says. "I know that you love her, but it simply was not meant to be. You must come to terms with that."

"I want to hear from the seers," I say sharply.

She doesn't say anything more to me. She just nods and walks to the door to let the seers in. Since they've been there this whole time, I imagine she expected this response from me.

They step in, dressed in their black robes, their faces stern. They all remain standing, waiting for my command.

I don't know what I expected to hear from them. Mother would not lie, and the seers' word is the most trusted among us. It would be foolish to doubt them, as they have always been the backbone of our pack. "I am meant to marry another?" It sounds more like a statement than a question. "The Chosen One?"

They all nod their heads in unison, and my heart sinks. I think of Rhiannon as all the hopes and dreams I had for our life together vanish before my eyes. I feel like I'm going to vomit.

"Lord," one of them says, "we need to act now if we want to rescue the girl. We may not have this chance again. Surely you understand how important this is for the pack."

"As long as she remains imprisoned," another says, "her life is in danger. We must act immediately or else our chance will be lost."

I narrow my eyes, suddenly feeling like there's a part of this I've missed. I look at Mother, who simply fills in, "I have not had the opportunity to tell him about her capture."

"The Chosen One?" I say. "She is the one who has been captured?"

"Yes, my Lord," the first seer says. "She has been taken by the Gorg pack in the name of the Shamans they serve."

"We were able to track them when they lowered their cloak to take her from the outer world," says the second seer. "The connection has been broken already, but we know their location as of twenty minutes ago. Assuming they have not gone far, we might just be able to get the girl out alive if we act immediately."

The Gorg Pack. They were a pack of rogue wolves left over from the great wars during the beginning of my cousin's reign as the Alpha King. Of the many rival packs in this region, they were the most dangerous because of their allegiance with the Shamans. And now they have the one person who can lift the curse that plagues us. I can't imagine what they were promised to help the Shamans, especially since the curse affects them as well.

It's also not lost on me that this is the way I'm told about my betrothal. I'm starting to wonder how long Mother knew before this creature was captured and forced her hand. Still, however I've found out about her, it's now my time to act.

"Fine," I say to them. "I'll gather who I need and move immediately. I will need two seers to accompany us." I point to two of them randomly, and they step out of the line. "You're with me. Let's get going before dark."

I walk out, the two seers on my heels. My mother calls after me, "Be safe!"

As I go, I already knowing who I want to join me. We need a small team. The goal is to get in and out quickly. I don't need all the clunky movements of our guards.

The pack is lounging in the open field just beyond the courtyard. I approach them, my seers flanking me. As I pass by, I catch a glimpse of Rhiannon as she stands off to the side. Seeing me move with intention, her instincts kick up and she stiffens, cocking her head as if asking to assist.

I'm not ready to face her right now. Not when I'm still trying to process the news myself. I walk away without acknowledging her, making my way to the other members of my pack.

Conan and Akila stand in one corner. Akila looks like she's tired of whatever it is Conan is trying to say to her and she would rather be somewhere else. Conan, my best friend, is a skilled fighter, but he loves to use his pretty boy face to charm every woman he comes across. He's been after Akila for some time now, but she hasn't given him the time of day, let alone her attention.

"Conan, Akila," I say, getting their attention. "I need you. Now."

"Finally. Something to do," Akila mutters as she stands and dusts herself off. Conan follows suit.

"Let's continue this later?" Conan smirks at Akila, but she just rolls her eyes and walks away from him.

"Let's not," she says.

"Where is Branson?" I ask them. I glance around for the big guy. He's a six-foot-seven-inch tower of a man with the strength of three regular wolves and among my top three best soldiers. I'm definitely going to need him.

"Last I saw, he was somewhere meditating," Akila says.

"Find him. We have a mission, and time is of the essence."

"Yes, my Lord," they say in unison. Akila rushes off toward the barracks. While we stand there, Rhiannon walks up behind me.

"Lord?" she says. "I will join you as well."

"No," I say. "I need the team to be small."

She blinks, an incredulous smile dancing at the corners of her lips. "But what's one more person? And I—"

"You heard me, Rhiannon," I growl it with warning. She knows better than to question me in front of everyone else. She sees the seriousness in my eyes and I see a bit of hurt in hers. Then she backs away.

"Yes, of course, Lord."

Akila comes running back with Branson right behind her less than a minute later, and we leave our fortress.

Chapter Three — Thea

I've been floating in and out of consciousness for who knows how long. The last thing I remember seeing is the dagger floating above me. I must have fainted. Every time I came to after, the man who was standing over me was gone, but the rest of them were still gathered around me, still chanting.

I'm awake again and fear has gripped me, along with the tightness of the rope around my body. My eyes flit around to the people dressed in white robes, their glowing, odd-colored eyes staring at me through the dim candlelit room.

I was walking home from work before this. Who . . . who are these people? Why are they trying to sacrifice me to whatever weird god they worship? My eyes start to burn with tears. "Please..." My voice is hoarse in my dry throat. I try again. "Please let me go."

This is just like the nightmares that keep plaguing me. Almost exactly. Down to the white robes and eerie chanting. Who would have thought they were real? My town really is killing me slowly, and now these scary people are going to make it quick.

The chanting stops, and one of them turns his head and says, "She is awake again."

"Please, please," I say frantically. "You have the wrong person. Just let me go."

A voice cuts me off. He leans in and says, "You are the Chosen One, and your sacrifice would be the saving grace for our people. You should count yourself lucky to be here."

I have no idea what he's talking about. How in the hell is this lucky? I was captured and taken against my will. Since when was being tied up with a dagger aimed at my chest supposed to be lucky?

"You have the wrong person," I say again. "I am not who you are looking for." I start to shake, tears and sweat flowing from my body in rivers.

Dear God, I'm not ready to die.

All my crying and pleading are falling on deaf ears as they start the chanting back up again. They're getting louder and louder. The one with the knife comes back. This time, he puts his hand on my arm and says, "I must ask you to stay conscious this time. You must be awake for the ritual to take."

I start breathing hard as he brings the knife up again over my heart. "No!" I cry out. "Please, don't!"

His hand raises sharply, readying to come back down on me.

A loud boom shakes the room, bringing in a strong wind and particles of earth scattering through the air all around me. I squeeze my eyes even tighter, wailing out in terror. I can't hear myself over the screams of the people around me, though. I force my eyes open, but it's pitch dark now. I can't see a thing.

All the candles have been blown out by the heavy wind, and I'm surrounded by foggy darkness. All I can see from my position on the slab are movements so fast that I only see them out of the corners of my eyes. Animal sounds and screams fill the room, piercing my ears as pandemonium erupts around me.

And then it all stops. I'm lying here, my body shaking violently from fear.

"Oh, well. That was fast," a gruff voice laments somewhere in the darkness. Slowly, I realize there are others here. Have . . . have they come to rescue me?

"They ran away with their tails tucked between their legs." This voice is a female one. I wonder how many are here now. Are my captors still here?

Four figures appear through the fog and walk toward where I lay, still tied up. Three men and one woman. Suddenly, I can see them clearly through the darkness . . . I don't know how, but my eyes focus in a way they never have before. I can see them perfectly as they walk up to me.

And one of them . . . I know him. I've seen his face before, but at the moment, I can't place where exactly. As he gets closer, it hits me. My dreams. Those eyes, blue with a silver ring around the irises, and the dark hair hanging in his face.

In my dreams, his eyes change from blue to gold, but not now. They're just blue and silver like I remember them.

"I'm dreaming," I say aloud. I have to be. None of this is real. I just have to wake . . . up . . . The last thing I hear before darkness claims me again is, "Did she just pass out after we saved her?"

The world comes back to me, and I'm met with those eyes again. I look over to see him looking down at me. He's focused on me with a deep-set frown on his face. The man from my dreams looks pissed.

"She's awake."

The tone of those two words does not inspire confidence. He sounds pretty annoyed that I have the nerve to be awake.

A middle-aged man in a white lab coat suddenly comes into my line of sight.

"Welcome back," he says in a bright voice. "It's good to see you here and alive." He's smiling at me, but I just stare skeptically. I refuse to believe that I'm out of danger yet. I won't let my guard down so easily. The past few hours have not been kind to me.

Wait. How long has it been since the people from the vehicle grabbed me off the street? I don't even know how long I've been missing. Surely, my coworkers will be looking for me by now.

I start crying. I don't know where I am or how long I've been here. I don't even know who these people are.

"Hey, hey. You're all right. You're safe." The doctor's voice is soft as he leans closer to comfort me. I try to move away, but he remains close. "I promise you. You are safe here. No harm will come to you."

If this is still a dream, I really want to wake up from it. It's gone on for much too long.

The doctor pulls a chair up to me, and that's when I notice I'm lying in a bed. The room is mostly white, but it's not a hospital . . . I don't think.

"You were injected with an unusually high dosage of poison," he explains. "The amount was more than . . . well, more than most people could withstand. You were able to survive, but I imagine you don't feel too great right now."

I shake my head. Now that he mentions it, my stomach feels sick. Like I had bad sushi.

A nurse comes in, and the man from my dreams steps out of the way so that she can hand the doctor a vial. "This should ease your nausea," he says and injects it into my arm before I can react. A warm feeling travels up my arm, and a second later, the nausea disappears.

Dream Man leans against the far wall, watching and frowning silently. For a handsome man, he sure frowns a lot. Or maybe the frown brings out his beauty.

"Who are you people?" I ask, my voice comes out croaky. "I can't still be dreaming, right?"

"Here, take gentle sips." The nurse is on the other side of me with a small cup and a straw.

I slowly lean up so I can drink what I hope is water. It certainly tastes like it, and my throat is soothed.

A rough scoff comes from Dream Man.

"You have got to be kidding me," he mutters and shakes his head. *What's he got to be so hostile about?*

My gaze shifts from him to others in the room to see if anyone has noticed how angry he is at me. No one's said anything. How rude is this guy?

"Take your time," the doctor says. "You'll need a little more rest to get your strength, but you should be right as rain soon."

"You haven't answered my question," I say to him. "Who are you? What am I doing here?"

The doctor looked over at Dream Man tentatively. "All will be revealed in due time," he said. "For right now, you should just concentrate on getting better."

"Weak." Dream man says it so soft that I could almost believe that I imagined it. He's just standing there like somebody pissed on his shoes, arms crossed, his mouth turned up with disgust.

"You know what? If you understood how my day has been," I snap at him, "you might be a little kinder. Being rude is really uncalled for right now."

It's like I dropped a bomb in the middle of the room. Both the doctor and the nurse freeze, eyes wide and fearful. The doctor dares a look back at Dream Man, who narrows his eyes at me as he stands up from the wall.

"You would do well to watch your tone," he growls at me. "I am Lord of this region. You will respect me."

"Respect is earned where I come from," I shoot back at him. He walks toward me, and the doctor tries to intervene.

"My Lord, please—"

"I am yet to see or understand why you are the Chosen One," he says through clenched teeth.

That phrase again. What in the world does that even mean? "You know, I don't know what you're talking about," I snap back at him, refusing to cower in his presence, "but so far, everybody that's called me that has only wanted to kill me. I'm starting to think that it's some kind of insult. So maybe you should watch your tone."

"You are a fool," he scoffs. "A silly girl from the outer lands. All these years of ancient wise men and seers, Shamans and Mages, all searching for *you?* It's ridiculous. You are clearly some kind of fraud."

My mouth hangs in shock. A *fraud*!

He turns to leave. "Fuck off, Fancy Pants," I spit at him. He whirls around.

This time, the doctor speaks up before Dream Man can do anything, "My Lord, please. She needs her rest and we have to consider what's at stake here. You should probably let us handle this for now."

He glares at me, silvery blue eyes raging with anger. "Fine. I need to speak with Mother and the seers about this travesty, anyway."

As he leaves, all I can think is What in the ever living hell is going on, and why have I been thrust into the middle of it?

"I am sorry," the doctor says after he's gone. "This is a . . . tense situation. I do apologize for Lord Xander's behavior."

I scoff. "Don't apologize. That guy's a dick."

"That *guy* is our Alpha, my dear. What he says goes around here."

I huff bitterly. The nurse excuses herself, and I glance over at the doctor. "What's your name, doc?"

He smiles gently. "I am Cid Olcan. I serve as the healer for Crescent Pack. The nurse that was just here is Rudy. She will be back with some medication to help you rest while your body heals."

I nod. I'm grateful for some explanation, even though that wasn't a lot at all. Ugh, I feel like I've slipped into Wonderland.

"So, you said I was poisoned?"

He nods. "Your captors were using an herb in an effort to keep you conscious for their ritual. Your body must have resisted it to the point of frustration because you had quite a lot of it in your bloodstream. It's really a miracle that you are alive. But then, if it is true that you are the Chosen One, well, then it is no miracle at all."

"Can you tell me what this Chosen One business is all about?"

Rudy came walking back in with a needle in hand. She starts injecting it in the IV drip by my bed. "I could not explain it properly," Dr. Olcan says. "The lore of it all . . . Well, it was just told to me as a boy, as it has been for many of us. I could not do it justice. I'm certain that you will be told all when you've recovered. For now, just know that you are very special to us, and it is very important that you stay alive."

The medicine kicks in quick, and I start to get a little lightheaded.

"You will be okay as long as you rest and we can monitor your progress," he adds. I'm starting to drift off. I lean my head back against the pillow and let my heavy eyes start to close.

Right before I fall asleep, the door opens again, and two people in dark robes come walking in. "Please be careful," Dr. Olcan says. "She's still very weak."

"She will not be harmed," I hear as they stand over me, raising their hands above me.

Not again.

I'm too weak to speak or move. All I can do is watch them with hazy eyes as they wave their hands over me.

Chapter Four — Xander

I still can't see it. I just don't see what others are seeing, and I can't imagine how she could possibly be the Chosen One.

By the time we brought her back, word had already gotten out that the Chosen One was among us and that we would all be saved. In town, everyone's been walking around with smiles on their faces, the cloud of doom that has been looming over the townspeople's heads for the past few years starting to fade away.

Everyone's hopes have been lifted. Except mine. But then, I'm one of the few who've actually met her. I should be the one most convinced, and I'm not. Maybe it's because I'm the only one who has lost so much already. I can't really bear to lose more.

Her insolence plagues me. I had to walk out of the infirmary before my wolf came out and ripped her to bits. I see nothing special in this girl. She's merely a random human who just so happened to be picked up off the streets and brought to Clarion. Even though the seers have confirmed who she is, I can't come to terms with it.

Why does it have to be this way?

"Did you plan on telling me, or was I just supposed to find out through gossip?"

My pace is stopped as Rhiannon's voice echoes around me in the hall. I turn to see her standing at a corner of the hallway, arms crossed, eyes blazing with anger and hurt.

I don't have anything to say. What can I say? I won't deny that I delayed speaking to her. I'm still trying to cope with it myself. She uncrosses her arms and steps up to me.

"Was that why you didn't take me with you on the rescue mission?" she asks. "Because of her?"

I want to wrap my hands around her beautiful face and tell her that it'll be all right. Tell her anything to ease her mind. But there isn't a single thing I can say that will remove the fact that I am fated to another.

"I am sorry," I say, doing my best to keep my own anger and rage out of my voice. "I never planned for any of this to happen—"

"You don't have to marry her," she says with water standing in her eyes. "You are the Alpha of this pack and this region. You... you can make whatever rules you want. We don't have to do this."

My mouth goes dry. "I don't have a choice."

"You always have a choice!" she shouts. "Isn't that what you used to tell me? We are not beasts. We are thoughtful, sentient beings and we always have a choice!" The hall is echoing with her voice and all the pain in it is echoing back at me. I stand there, letting her hurt spill out before me, helpless to do anything to stop it.

"You don't have to do this," she says in a small voice. "Xander...we don't have to accept this."

"But we do." I pause, my mind reverting to duty. Always to duty when things get hard. It's my safety net. It always has been. "Rhiannon, you have to understand, as the Alpha there have to be sacrifices. The pack comes first. My region comes *first*. You do realize that, don't you?"

She doesn't say anything. She stands there, shaking with grief and anger. The standing water in her eyes quivers and rolls down her cheeks. "Yes." Her voice is starting to break. "Yes, but not like this." She walks toward me and puts her hands on my face. I inhale her scent, the memories of our love rising up within me.

"I love you, Xander," she says, tears rolling down her face in rivers now. "I have loved you since we were children. Do you not love me?"

"Of course, I love you."

"Then let's leave. We can go somewhere else where no one knows us and build the family we both want. Let's leave this cursed place and start over. Somewhere far from Clarion altogether."

"We cannot leave," I tell her. "This pack . . . our families are here. We cannot abandon them. Not at any cost."

"We are cursed," she hisses. "The wolves of this region have been killing each other for ages. We are doomed, Xander. We always have been. We should be using this time to escape, not pin our hopes on some . . . some ancient myth."

This hurts so much. I hear her pain and I want her words to be real. I want to run away with her more than anything.

"We can leave," she goes on. "It doesn't have to be this way."

"The curse will follow us and I know you don't really want that." I take her hands and pull them from my face, pushing them down to her sides. She snatches them away.

"You are the only thing I want. How can you expect me to go on serving this pack as I watch you live your life with another woman? You cannot ask that of me."

"I must," I say. "I am your Alpha, and what I do, I do for the good of us all. It is as simple as that. Would you have us run off like that girl's parents did so long ago? We are not the cowards they were."

Hurt fills her face, the word *coward* like a slap. I wish I could take her pain away.

"I cannot turn my back on my pack, Rhiannon," I add through clenched teeth. "You know me better than that."

Her nostrils flare. She steps away from me and says, with so much anger, "Fine. Do what you want. Go be with your Chosen One, and I hope you have a better life with her." She turns and stalks away from me . . . perhaps forever.

I watch her leave until she's out of my sight. Then, I turn and walk away, my mind starting to spin. I have duties to attend to, and maybe I should start thinking of a way out of this. Surely, there must be something somewhere.

We have had a strange issue with the population recently. I had intended to dedicate some time to researching it. Perhaps I will also spend that time finding a loophole to get me out of this disaster.

"So, I've heard congratulations are in order."

I'm sitting in the living room, books all around me as I'm trying to find some hole or some bit of lore that has been overlooked. My brother, Luther, stands in my door, looking at me with a smirk on his face.

"Where have you been?" I ask him. "I would have liked you with me in the rescue party."

He shrugs, walking in casually as he does everywhere he goes. Luther always walks like he's got nowhere to be. "I've been around. Besides, you're the Alpha, not me. No one cares where I am or what I'm doing. It's the many perks of being the spare. I can come and go as I please."

I just grunt as I turn back to my books. Luther's way has always been to drift in and out of rooms and conversations. I'd say it was normal, but lately, he's been making fewer and fewer appearances around our den.

He sighs and drops on the couch next to me. I glance over at him. "You know, there's a rumor going around that you're hanging out with the Gorg pack."

He snorts a laugh. "As if I would ever be seen with those smelly animals."

"You laugh, but people talk when you make it a point not to be around when things get hairy around here. You should make more of an effort."

"Yes, my Alpha," he says, a twinge of sarcasm in his voice. "So, have you seen her? Does she have bright lights around her like the stories we had been told?" His eyes gleam sardonically. I just throw him a dry look.

"Ah. No bright lights," he says. "Okay. What about the change? She has turned, hasn't she?" He whistles in false amazement before I can answer him. "Half Shaman, half wolf. Now, *that* would be a sight."

"It certainly would."

He glances over at me, then lifts the book I have in my lap to see the cover. I snatch it away from him, but the damage is already done. He laughs and shakes his head. "*Legends and Myths of Clarion*. Interesting. Looking for a loophole, I see. What do you think you'll find that the seers have not?"

"I don't know," I reply tensely. "But I can't sit around here and do nothing. Besides, that's not all I'm looking for." I reach for one of the other books and toss it to him. He catches it and, frowning, looks skeptically at the cover.

"You're . . . studying the population?"

"It's increasing, if you can believe that. There's something happening in this town, and I need to find out what."

He nods. "Right. Say, why don't you go for a run with me? We can find some other pack members and make an evening out of it. Get your mind off your worries."

"I'll pass."

"You're troubled," he says. "You need fresh air and a good, hard run. Maybe even a hunt. You're going to burn yourself out if you sit here all night like this."

I sigh and close the book on my lap, rubbing the bridge of my nose. "Rhiannon found out about it through the rumor mill."

Luther's face drops a little. "Oh. She confronted you?"

I nod slowly, remembering the hurt on her face. "I could do nothing to comfort her. How could I? This is bigger than us."

His eyes glance down at the book in my lap, "Unless you can find a way out of it."

I set the book aside. "I know there's no way out. I just wish . . . I don't know what I wish."

My brother pats me on the shoulder and says, "Take a break with me. You can come back to this right after if you like. You need to do something other than fretting over your responsibilities."

I smile at him. My younger brother looks back at me with a nearly identical face. Blue and silver eyes and dark hair that's a little longer than mine. "Thank you," I tell him, "but I'm fine. Truly."

"All right." He sits back, then claps his hands and stands up. "I am off to go introduce myself to my sister-in-law-to-be and maybe charm her into being my mate instead. That ought to help, right?"

I turn a sharp gaze at him.

"Kidding," he says, putting his hands up defensively. "I'll see you around, Alpha."

He leaves, and I turn my attention back to the books that are currently in front of me. The increase in our numbers is puzzling, and I haven't determined yet if it's something to be worried about. Since the beginning of the curse, we've been keeping other residents of Clarion out for everyone's safety. Perhaps this was an increase in births, though why anyone would have whelps now is beyond me.

Once upon a time, we had people coming from all over to build a life here. This used to be a common place for people to settle. And with every new resident, we updated countless logs to record our growth.

As a pup, I used to sit with my father as he sifted through records. Being the lesser child of a royal birth, he had spent much of his education with numbers and patterns, whereas my uncle focused on his duties as Alpha King of Clarion. When my father came to this region and began to build the town from the ground up, he took pride in every step in our path to becoming a great city. That all seems like a lifetime ago now. Whenever things get tough or I find myself at a crossroads, the pup I once was wishes I could go to my father for guidance.

"My Lord." I look up at the two elders standing at the door with more books in their hands. "We have the list from two months ago."

"Please, come in."

"Son? Wake up, my dearest."

I open my eyes to see Mother standing over me. She's touching my face gently. I sit up and look around, a million opened books all around me.

"It's very late," she says, moving a few books next to me and sitting down. "What are you looking for?"

I yawn, sleep still hovering over me. "Trying to busy myself by solving a problem. The population increase."

She chuckles. "It's not uncommon for populations to increase during times of strife. You don't need all these books to know that."

I nod, and my mind goes back to my first meeting with the Chosen One. A sick feeling comes over my stomach.

"I don't know that I can do this," I say to her softly. She pauses in question, then nods in understanding. "Rhiannon, she was . . . she is everything to me."

Mother reaches over and squeezes my hand. "She will always mean something to you. That will not change, my dear."

She doesn't say anything for a long time, then, "When your father died, I thought I would die with him. I did not think that I had anything left to do anymore because he was my entire world. The pain and despair drove me to find battles to fight or problems to solve. I started questioning everything. I questioned life and death, the Moon Goddess. Everything. And then, one day, you asked me if we were ever going to see him again. I looked into your eyes, your father's eyes, and I thought that I could see him already. I believe I told you as much."

I smile and she smiles back. "You did not lose Rhiannon the way I lost your father, but the life you had and the love you shared will always be with you. One day, you will use it to build a new life that you never expected you'd have. I know it because you are your father's son, Xander, and you are my son. Life may not go according to plan right now, but like your father, you will work your way through, always keeping the intentions of your family in mind."

She leans her head to mine, and I close my eyes, grateful for her presence. "Every member of our pack has a role to play," she says softly, "some more significant than others. Yours is one of true sacrifice, and it's not to be taken lightly."

She pulls away and pats me on the cheek. "So, have you spoken to her?"

I exhale a deep breath. "Not since she first arrived. I may have said some things to her out of anger."

She chuckles lightly. "This is a whole new territory for her. The seers say she does not understand anything at the moment, so she needs all the help she can get. And there's no one better than you to give it to her, don't you think?"

She's right. Thea was just plucked out of one world and dropped into another. As angry as I was, I wasn't angry with her. Not really. I can't imagine what all this must be like for her.

"So speak to her again," Mother says, "and when you do, extend some grace."

Chapter Five — Thea

"She needs rest. All of this is overwhelming for her. We cannot have all of you crowding in like this." The first thing I hear when I open my eyes is Nurse Rudy reprimanding some people on the other side of the wall.

Since regaining consciousness *again*, I've gained some of my strength back. I've also been getting a lot of visitors. Strange people of all different ages have been coming in and treating me like I'm some sort of discovery. Some came and stood by the door, peering at me like I was going to bite them if they got too close. Others stared like I was supposed to have a horn growing out of my forehead or something. I tried to be as kind as I possibly could. I even tried to offer thanks to Rudy for keeping things down to a dull roar so that I could get the rest I needed.

Once, a cute little girl came in to ask if I brought light whenever I wanted to turn. When I asked her what I was supposed to turn into, she giggled and told me I was funny.

I truly wish I was that funny in that moment, but the truth is that I had never been more serious in my life.

When Rudy comes back in, I'm going to ask her to explain all this to me once and for all. This is getting ridiculous.

The door finally opens, and I roll over, expecting to see Rudy. Instead, I'm met with a man who looks vaguely familiar. He's handsome. Long dark hair, blue eyes with silver rings around them. Oh . . . he looks like the grumpy Dream Man from earlier. But it's definitely not him. This man is smiling pleasantly. Easily, even. Like he's just come back from vacation.

"The Chosen One in the flesh," he says casually. "It's an honor." He bows. Like, literally bows his head, Englishman style.

I just tip an eyebrow up at him. His smile broadens at my expression.

"Was that too much?" he asks.

"Unless this is the end of act one, yeah. I'd say it is."

He laughs. "I like your sense of humor. We will be great friends."

There's something about him that sets my senses off. I've always believed that I could sense when someone was hiding something or just when someone seemed off. Ethan used to say that I have a sixth sense about people. This person standing in front of me, although charming, definitely has something he's hiding, and he's trying to mask it with charm.

"I am Luther, Xander's brother," he says. I blink silently at him, having no idea who he's talking about. He adds, "You may have seen him since he brought you here. The Alpha?"

Chosen One, Alpha, seers . . . Doesn't anybody have normal a title around here?

"Ah," he says, waving my confusion away with a sweep of his hand. "You'll get used to everyone soon enough. I just wanted to introduce myself to you since we're going to be family."

"Luther, dear. Let the girl be."

A beautiful woman walks through the door and steps into the room. She's the most beautiful woman I have ever seen. She has high cheekbones like a model and wide blue eyes. Her golden hair frames her face and falls down to her waist.

"I'm just getting to know her," Luther replies. "I tried to stop by last night, but Olcan's guard dog wouldn't let me in."

She smiles gently at him, patting him on the shoulder as she walks in. "Well, I think you've had enough time with her. Yes?"

Luther doesn't put up any argument. He just winks at me before turning to walk out. Before he goes, he stops and kisses the woman on the cheek.

"I am Gemma," she says to me after he's gone. She walks right up to the bed, seeming to float all the way, too, the hem of her long, gold-trimmed gown sweeping the floor without any sign of movement of her feet.

As soon as she gets close to me, a strange feeling of familiarity comes over me. There's something soothing about her presence.

"May I?" she gestures to the space on my bed.

I nod and shift over to make more space for her.

"How do you feel?" she asks as she sits.

"Better, thank you." I find it very interesting that, save for the doctor and the nurse who treated me, she's the only person who has bothered to ask how I'm doing.

"That's good," she responds.

"I'm just a little confused still. Nobody will tell me what I'm doing here or what all this is about. Everybody keeps coming in here like I'm some kind of celebrity. You know, I think you have the wrong person. I'm no Chosen One or anything of that sort. I'm just a regular girl who was walking home from work before I got dragged here, wherever here is. You know, I was almost killed, and then saved, and then I was brought here . . ." I put my hands to my face, trying not to break down. "I'm just confused as hell, and I want to go home."

Gemma smiles at me the whole time as I spill my guts to her. Then she puts a hand on my knee.

"First, allow me to assure you that you are no regular girl. You are here because this is where you should be. Where you should have been a long time ago. You should think of this as your homecoming."

Homecoming? That is so strange I can't even process it.

"Tell me, are there things that you are able to do that others may have found different?"

I have an immediate urge to say no, but I stop myself. There are many things that I can do that I've never talked about to anyone. I swallow hard and say tentatively, "There are . . . a few things. I mean, nothing big. Sometimes, I can feel when people are full of shit, for example. Once in a while I can sense when someone I know is coming to visit. Things like that."

She chuckles delicately. It's a disarming sound, and I want to go on. "And sometimes, I can hear people through walls or even people who are far away from me. And sometimes . . . well, I guess I have déjà vu." She frowns a little, so I add, "Like I know when something's about to happen."

She nods slowly. "Interesting. You should know that, here, you are not alone in what might be considered strange where you came from. For example, I am a Lycan. More commonly known as a werewolf."

I stare at her, trying to understand what she just said. *Lycans. Wolves.*

"Some of us are hybrids of other creatures. It is extremely rare, though."

It sounds like bullshit. Werewolves? Seriously. Yet, her sincerity has me intrigued. I lean in, fascinated. "Why would that be rare? Do people not . . . mix well here?"

She shakes her head slowly. "The mating of wolf and Shaman is strictly prohibited. In other parts of Clarion, similar unions are more accepted. In fact, our king recently mated with a young Phoenix, one of the rarest among us."

Okay. *What?* My mind is spinning. Clarion? Phoenix? "I'm . . . I'm sorry. I know you're trying to explain things to me, but...I feel like you're talking another language or something. Werewolves, Phoenixes, none of that is real."

"Oh, but they are. *We* are very real, my dear."

I nod slowly. "And…and what does any of this have to do with me?

"My dear," she says in her gentle tone, "you are a Daywolf. A very special and rare being. Your kind only exists once in many generations, if ever at all. Daywolves are like Lycans in the way that they can turn from wolf to human and back again…but they are also so much more. They carry the abilities of Shaman."

"What are Shaman? And what do you mean by 'rare'?"

She takes in a breath and suddenly, I have the feeling that there's a lot that I'm about to hear. "There is much about us that you have to learn. But the important thing to know is that you…your kind…well, they are not meant to exist. Daywolves are usually creatures spoken about only in myth in legend. And they are a *very* powerful breed."

"Why . . . why aren't we meant to exist?"

"Lycan and Shaman cannot mate. Physically, it's thought to be impossible. Lycan are made to change forms and Shaman…well, they appear human, but mostly, it is said that they are made of light and shadow. Some have said that Shaman have no form at all and only appear as human when they need to. No one could imagine that two such beings could ever mate. And yet, here you are." She says the last part with a smile. I reach over and pinch myself. This has to be another dream.

"Indulge me for a moment, Thea," she says, taking my hand and placing it between hers. "I want to tell you a story. For as long as the oldest Lycan can remember, we have been at war with the Shamans. Some creatures are just not meant to co-exist. That is just the nature of things. So this hatred passed on from one generation to the next until we all forgot how the war began. In a bid to move forward, the Lycans and Shamans proposed peace to one another. To seal the treaty between our people, a marriage was arranged between a male wolf and a Shaman woman to form this alliance. To solidify this union, the Shaman agreed to live among the wolf packs."

"Sounds dangerous," I say softly.

"Well, at first, things were going well. The newlyweds were living peacefully together, and all seemed to work out between our factions. And then rumors got out that the newlyweds weren't getting along. Those rumors started to prove real, and both families stepped in to help solve their problems. As wolves tend to be most loyal to their own kind, they stood fully behind their kindred, seeing the problem to be with the Shaman woman. That enraged her and her family. Distrust grew between the families . . . and the young couple."

"She suffered in silence for a while, but eventually, she could no longer stand to be around her husband or his family. That turned into a terrible hate within her, which led to her cursing the wolves within our region. All who would be born here, all who would die here, every wolf who came to be from that point on, would suffer for holding a loyalty to only their own. The curse pit wolf against wolf. Neighbors who had known each other for generations suddenly detested one another. Mothers and daughters, fathers against sons, brothers against brothers, all found themselves at odds. And every full moon, that hatred spills over in our streets."

"That's . . . that's horrible," I whisper.

"It gets worse," Gemma continues. "The Shaman vowed that the night of the Moon Comet would culminate in an end of all wolf kind in this region. Any wolf who shares the bloodline of the wolves that lived long ago will engage in a bloody war that will destroy us all."

I don't know what to say. It's a fantastic story, one that she clearly believes wholeheartedly, and, for some reason, I believe as well. "When is the Moon Comet supposed to come?" I ask her.

"In a few months' time," she says. "But there is hope. Perhaps as a way to seal our fates, she made one single decree. The curse could be broken by the offspring of a

Shaman and a wolf. You see now, how that was a clever trick, since a Shaman and a wolf are not thought to be able to bear children."

I frown at her, a slow understanding of what she's saying coming through to me. She continues, "We thought we were lost. As the night of the Moon Comet approaches, the outbursts around the city have become more and more violent. We have walled off and strengthened the borders to protect the rest of Clarion, for any wolf who joins the bloodline of the original cursed ones will be cursed as well. We have lived in isolation for centuries."

I don't have anything to say to that. A heaviness fills me. How lonely it must be to spend one's life in the place they were born. I think about where I just came from and shudder at the idea of never being able to leave.

"And then," she goes on, "more than two decades ago, a Shaman and a wolf mated in secret and conceived. As we understand it, they were found out shortly after the birth of the child. The mother, a Shaman, decided to hide her baby among the humans—the last place Shamans or Lycans would go looking. And it worked well for many years until this child was found and captured by both Shamans and an enemy wolf pack. The Shamans realized that the coming of the Moon Comet meant the end of all wolves in this region, so they enlisted the help of the Gorg Pack to find and kill our only savior."

Chills run all over my body. "Me. I was the one who was supposed to die."

She nods. "Thanks to our seers, who never stopped searching, we were able to find and save you before it was too late. And we mean to protect you from those who might harm you. You're too important to us."

I sit in silence, processing what she's told me. It's so hard to believe, but it explains everything. The men with the knife. The people coming to see me. Everything. I put my face in my hand and chuckle. It's a hollow sound. There's nothing funny about any of this.

"You know," I say to her, "I used to have this reoccurring dream where I would see myself tied up and about to be killed before being saved by a handsome stranger. Then when I was captured, I was in the exact same place, and everything was happening exactly like my dreams . . . and then the same man came in and saved me."

"Xander?" she asks.

"I don't know. I think so. The other one, um, Luther mentioned him earlier. If he's the same guy that was here before him, pardon my French, but he was a grade-A asshole."

She laughs that silver bell laugh again. "My son has his bad days."

I freeze.

"Your *son*?" I gape at her in disbelief and a bit of embarrassment.

"Yes. The Alpha. He's my son."

Oh my days. I just sat here and insulted her son.

"I am so sorry," I stammer, backtracking. "I didn't mean—"

"Oh, please," she says with a good-natured wave of her hand. "He might be my son, but he is far from perfect."

She seems to be taking this all in stride, but my face is flushing a million shades of red right now.

She pats my hand gently and says, "We are here to show you and guide you. Everyone you come into contact with will, in their own way, help you to achieve your fullest potential. Come." She stands up from the bed. "Do you think you can stand?"

"Uh, I think so." I push myself off the bed, and she helps me stand. It feels so good to have my legs on the ground. "Where are we going?" I ask.

"It is time I tell you all about the people you will call family. I don't know if you have noticed, but they are eager to meet you."

"Family? Oh, well, that's, um, interesting."

She pauses, cocking her head slightly. Then her blue eyes widen as she gasps. "Oh, dear. You don't know. Well, of course you don't. With my son being so terrible to you, I'm sure he neglected to inform you."

"Inform me of what?"

"Well, that you two are to be mated."

I laugh. She's joking. The way she said that was so casual, it has to be a joke. She tightens her hand on mine and leads me out of the room. I guess it's off to meet my "family," whoever that is.

Chapter Six — Thea

By my count, I'd say that it's been about a week since I arrived here, and apart from the shocking turn of events, the public response to me has been very welcoming. At least for the majority of them. It's weird how I was a complete stranger to everyone here, yet ever since I arrived, I've been made to feel at home. During my time in the infirmary, I received gifts and visitors almost every day, many of them thanking me for some deed I have yet to perform. They all regard me with such hope that I've been doing my best to hide the swirling doubt inside me.

This is such a strange place, and I don't know the details of how it exists or even where it is in relation to the small town I came from, but never in a million years would I have ever imagined that I would be here.

For one thing, the Lycans are so strange and beautiful, especially in wolf form. After Dr. Olcan approved my release, Gemma came to me and took me on a walk around the grounds. I saw people walking with wolves so large they almost rivaled small horses. Like that was normal! Gemma saw how taken aback I was. I guess it's hard to hide how unsettling giant wolves are when you just see them walking around in the wild like that.

The wolf people are *fast* and incredibly agile. On that walk, we stopped and watched children play ball in the courtyard. The way they moved, like they were lighter than air, defying the laws of physics in the speed at which they ran with the ball from one end of the area to the other. It was amazing.

"They only seem amazing now," Gemma had said, "but wait. You will be as fast as them very soon. Perhaps even faster."

I was only vaguely sure of what that meant, and at the time, I merely nodded and smiled.

If there's one thing I do know now as I take my daily walk around the courtyard, and that is that this is a community that lives as one. I have never felt more at peace. For the first time in a while, I haven't had to worry about work or scraping enough money together for rent or food. This life is freer than anything I have ever known.

If I had ever tried to imagine what a wolf pack home would look like, I never would have imagined this place. It's a large expanse of land and everyone seems to have their own buildings. It's almost like a trailer park or perhaps a community structure of some sort, but more refined. Still, as large as this place is, they seem to be entirely cut off from the world. It makes me wonder what's outside of this place. Gemma tells me that it's this way for the safety of all of Clarion—which, as it turns out, is what this land or city is called.

There's still a lot I don't know, but I think I'm getting the hang of how things are. I have Gemma and many of the townspeople to thank for that. They've made me feel at home here.

And then there's Xander. I see him walk out of one of the buildings, a permanent scowl on his face. He hardly ever speaks to me, and whenever I feel his eyes on me, the look he gives me is less than kind. Not disgust, but . . . I don't know. Angry disappointment, perhaps.

And yet I find myself attracted to him. Just as I had when he was in my dreams, even when he was standing in the infirmary scowling and complaining. There's something in the way he walks with intention. He takes strong strides like he knows exactly who he is in this place. I watch him now, his dark hair shining in the sunlight, the silver in his eyes glinting as he turns his head toward where the pack is training.

If only he wasn't such a fucking asshole.

And as it turns out, Gemma wasn't joking about us being betrothed. I don't know how that's supposed to happen since we can barely tolerate each other.

According to Gemma, we are to be married by the next full moon, which was coming up faster than I can keep up with everyone's names and faces. Once we're mated, I should be able to activate my powers after we've consummated our marriage. I look out at him, walking away from me. He's got a nice ass, I'll admit, but a nice ass alone does not make me eager to have sex with him. This whole thing sounds like something from the Victorian Era.

I hope the seers won't be there to stand and watch, too, I think with a shudder.

To make matters worse . . . well . . . I've never even had sex before. The only intimate thing I had ever done with a boy was kiss. Which was actually a dare at a friend's party I once sneaked out to attend. My adopted parents were fiercely Christian and watched me like a hawk when I got to be a teenager. They enrolled me in every after school activity there was and made sure I was just too busy to date...which I was. The end result was me graduating at the top of my class, yet having no inclination to be anything more than just a waitress.

It's funny how once I got out in the world, I realized how small my life was and instantly longed for a change. And once I was set on that...well...I just never had the opportunity or the inclination to date. I'd hoped that one day, I'd have sex with someone I cared for. I'd even started to think that maybe I might find somebody once I moved out on my own. Not this archaic arranged marriage shit.

I never believed in love at first sight. But as my feelings for Xander stand right now, I totally believe in hate at first sight.

"Are you anticipating the next full moon like the rest of the pack?" A voice joins me on my walk. A familiar yet uncomfortable voice that makes me wary. I glance over to see that it's Luther, Xander's brother. He tends to pop up in places I happen to be, which is probably a coincidence. It still creeps me out a little.

I smile politely at him. "Yeah, kind of," I answer.

"You certainly don't sound so sure." He gives me a smirk. He is a handsome man like Xander. Looks a lot like him, too, except his hair is a little longer and his face a little rounder. "Are you getting cold feet? You know it is completely okay if you don't think you are up for the task."

I snort a laugh. "You're saying that like either of us has some kind of choice. Last I heard, I'm destined to marry your brother."

He nods. "Well, we are the masters of our own destiny, are we not?" He raises an eyebrow, his smirk gone. "I understand how all of this can feel like a burden, and even though every other person here has told you how you will help lift the curse, you shouldn't feel pressured into doing it. You can do whatever you like in the end."

I stop my walk and look up at him curiously. I knew there was a reason he makes me uncomfortable. "You don't approve of his union, do you?" I say.

Luther seems to always have a joyful look on his face. Always seems to be joking. Not right now. He stares down at me with eyes that feel like daggers. "Does that matter? What I think is irrelevant, but I'll tell you something, Thea, if it were me, I would be hard-pressed to marry someone I didn't love, or let alone like very much."

I stiffen and take an involuntary step back. "All of this is new territory for me, but I think I can handle it."

He stares for a long moment, then he smiles, his dark eyes relaxing. It's like a mask has slid back on. He glances over my shoulder and says, "Well, would you look at that."

"What?" I look over my shoulder and follow his line of sight.

Xander's standing with two other guys and a girl. They all look to be about my age, maybe a little older. I recognized them as the Xander's soldiers or warriors or whatever. I sometimes see them patrolling the halls or the grounds around my quarters. It looks like they'd been training a few minutes ago, and now they're watching us. Xander's sour face looks even more sour than usual.

"Oh, I think someone is not happy seeing us together." Luther says with a chuckle..

I scoff and turn away. "Xander *never* looks happy when he sees me."

"One could hardly blame him given that his former betrothed has been kicked to the side."

I look up at him, my stomach tightening. "What?"

He nods toward the group, and I look again at the three of them. The woman turns away, tying her reddish-brown hair up as she says something to Xander with a sneer.

"That is the ravishing Rhiannon," says Luther, "the girl who captured Xander's heart . . . and vice versa."

Oh. I feel my cheeks get warm with embarrassment.

"They had been together since childhood," he goes on, "even thought they would be mates. Too bad that just wasn't meant to be."

Looking at them, they would have been quite the pair. I've never met Rhiannon. Never even really seen her around much, but I feel terrible for her. I wish I could tell her that none of this was my intention. If I had it my way, I'd be halfway to New York or California by now.

Left to me, I would never be mates with someone who also hated my guts.

"But then," Luther adds, "we are the masters of our own destiny. Are we not?"

I look over at him, smiling in the jovial way that he does. He walks away without another word, and my stomach twists into a knot. I get his implication, but I don't believe he's suggesting it for my sake. He's clearly got another agenda in mind.

When I look back at Xander, he's turned away from me, waving to the others to go back to training. He didn't seem to be too keen on Luther being near me either. Maybe he feels the same way I do about his brother. Guess I'll never know for sure.

And so . . . it's my wedding day. Or whatever this is.

I'm standing in front of a tall mirror as I look at myself in my wedding dress, if you could call it that. It's not large or white or even grand in any way. It's simple and beige and flows down past my feet. It's got intricate decoration embroidered in the hem and sleeves, but for all intents and purposes, this has more in common with a christening gown.

At least it matches my hair color, kind of. All this off white is making my platinum locks look glowy, or maybe it's just the sunlight coming in through the window making it all look that way.

My fingers rub the fabric of the dress as I nibble on my lips, my stomach turning.

"You look beautiful, Thea." Gemma's voice speaks behind me. I look at her in the mirror.

"Thanks." I give her a small smile. "What if this doesn't work?" I blurt out.

She looks at me for a moment, then takes me by my shoulders. "Just have faith, my dear. All will be well once the ceremony is done."

I don't know what she means or even what is going to happen. I keep imagining that I'm going to burst into a ball of light or something the second the ceremony is done.

She turns me around and spends a little time fussing with my hair. Then, the door to the little room we're in opens, and one of Xander's pack peeks her head in. She's got long auburn braids, dark eyes, and a very kind smile. I think her name is Akila.

"We're ready, Madam," she says to Gemma. Her eyes shift to me, and her smile fades a little. "Is she all right?"

"I'm fine," I say. "Let's get this over with."

Gemma steps back and grabs the veil sitting off to the side. The veil, just a twisty ring of branch and vine with sheer beige cloth all around it, is placed on my head and over my face. She smiles at me from the other side of the fabric.

"Let the ceremony begin," she says.

I'm led out into the courtyard, and immediately, I see the other members of the pack standing in a line leading to a carriage. It doesn't look all that fancy, really. A dark box on wooden wheels. As I walk out with Gemma's arm around me, I glance at the subjects gathered in the courtyard, excitement on their faces. None of them can reach me at all as the largest of the pack stands guard around us.

Gemma, Akila, and I get into the carriage, and we're moving in no time. I ask Gemma, "Why the heavy guard? I thought everyone wanted this."

"These are uncertain times," she says. "We can't leave anything to chance."

We ride for a short time. There are no windows, so I can't see anything as we go, but I hear the noises of people just outside. Cheers? Are people waiting on the side of the road for us to pass? I wish I could see them.

When the carriage stops, the door opens, and the largest man I've ever seen steps to the side so we can leave. This is the one that everyone calls Branson. A wall of a man who rarely speaks. He looks at us and nods his head. "Madam, this way."

I'm not sure who he's talking to, but we all get out. The second I step out into the moonlight, I'm shocked at my surroundings. We're standing at the edge of a long stone path in a field as large as a football field. Maybe larger.

And there are so many people. All of them are sitting on the grass, forming a giant, layered circle. Crowds of people look on as my grip on Gemma's arm tightens.

We walk down the stone path to the circle's center, a lush green field with the rays of the moon setting everything to a high glow. There is very little there, other than a man dressed in black robes and a stone altar with a chalice sitting on it.

And Xander. Of course, Xander. He looks very handsome, wearing a loose shirt with the top three buttons open. His hair is shorter, slicked back, and definitely groomed for this wedding. As we approach, I catch sight of his blue eyes, glowing like jewels under the moonlight.

And he's not scowling. Not tonight. He just gazes at me with a look I can't explain.

I reach the altar. Gemma and Akila both kneel on either side of me. The man in the robe begins the ceremony with, *We are here to join these two under the light of the Moon Goddess...*

My mind wanders as he drones on. As I gaze around myself, it looks like everyone in town has come to watch this ceremony, which isn't surprising. I'm supposed to save their world, right?

Xander takes my hand, and I snap back into the moment. From his hand, a black wolf's claw protrudes. He traces a line down the center of my palm, and I restrain the urge to laugh. It tickles terribly.

"You are mine," he says, "and I am yours. From now until eternity."

He releases my hand. Both the robed man and him look at me expectantly. Nervously, I take Xander's hand. My gaze falls on Luther, kneeling at his brother's side opposite Akila. *We are the masters of our own destiny...*

I look away. It's too late to back out now if I ever *was* going to. I clear my throat and run my nail down the center of his hand.

"Y-you are mine, and I am yours. From now until eternity."

Xander looks to the robed man as he takes both of our hands and raises them to the sky. "Let that which the Moon Goddess has called to fate never be torn asunder. You may partake of her libations."

Xander picks up the chalice and takes a short drink. Then he hands it to me, and I follow suit. It tastes like bitter red wine.

"And so, you are mated," says the robed man. The crowd around us erupts with joy. Xander forces a smile on his face and takes my hand, leading me back to the carriage.

―――ele―――

I guess this is Xander's bedroom. I look around and register how clean it is. It's not OCD-like, just uncluttered. Tidy, perhaps.

Xander walks in behind me and sits on the bed. He starts unbuttoning his shirt, and I'm frozen as I watch him reveal his muscular chest. I'm torn between my lust and fear, my feet wanting to run but having no direction.

We haven't spoken a single kind word since we met, and now we're in his room for the consummation. My heart is pounding so fast I think I might faint. He sighs.

"Come sit, Thea. The sound of your racing heart is unsettling."

I'm taken out of my fear for a moment. *Unsettling?*

Stiffly, I walk around to the other side of the bed and sit down, my back to him. The bed moves a little as he gets up and walks over to me. "That's not how it works, Thea." He stands over me. I'm not looking at him, but I can feel his eyes on me. "The consummation will not happen with you on the other side of the bed."

I fix my gaze straight ahead, not moving a muscle. He walks in front of me and kneels, reaching out and removing my veil. There's a flash of frustration in his eyes, but the way his hand moves over my head is gentle, as if he doesn't wish to disturb me.

"I'll be quick," he says softly. "If you wish, you can close your eyes until it's done."

He's . . . he sounds so kind. It's almost like someone switched Xanders on me. I take a deep breath and close my eyes. It takes a moment, but before long, I feel his hand gently move my hair away from my face, his lips on my neck. Warm and soft, the sensation sends a shiver through me, and a breath rushes out of my lips.

His mouth moves from my neck to my chin and then to my lips. At first, I can't understand what I'm feeling until he gently prods my lips open with his tongue, and I realize that I'm getting warm and wet between my legs.

I follow his lead, kissing him back as his tongue caresses mine. He gently pushes me down to the bed and pulls my dress up my thighs. Instinctively, my hands move to his chest. His pecs are firm under my fingertips.

He moves away for a moment, and I open my eyes in time to see him take off his pants. Then he's on top of me, his hands finding my breasts under the thin fabric of my gown as he maneuvers himself between my legs. I feel him, rock hard and ready, as he presses against my soaking wet center.

And then fear takes hold. I pull back, my arm stiffening against his chest. He looks down at me with confusion for a moment, then his eyes soften as he realizes.

"You've . . . never done this before?"

I shake my head.

He looks away for a moment, something unreadable in his eyes. He takes in a deep breath and says, "I'll go slow," he says. "Okay?"

I bite my lip and nod. This has to happen . . . so let it happen.

He enters me slowly. Pain and pleasure move through me, and I gasp sharply. He pauses, watching my face for any sign of my resistance before continuing. He caresses my face and kisses my lips softly, then continues, thrusting slowly and purposefully. The pain starts to give way to an intense pleasure, and I reach over and grab the sheets. He grabs hold of my hands and wraps them around him so that my hands are on his back.

"Dig into me," he growls. "Not the sheets. It will help you bear it."

"I—" I can't speak. The warm feeling is taking over everything inside me. The way I was gripping those sheets, I don't want to do the same to his back.

"Don't worry about hurting me," he adds.

My legs begin to shake as I obediently dig my nails into his skin. My moans mix with his low guttural growls, and suddenly, he closes his eyes, turning his head away from me. His thrusts get harder, and I feel myself start to explode from the inside.

"Oh . . . y-yes," I gasp, my voice sounding shaky and desperate. A rumble grows within him, and he lifts up, looking down at me with glowing gold eyes.

We both climax at the same time, my body shaking, giving into him. Stars flashed before my eyes, my toes curling.

For what it's worth, my first time turned out to be more amazing than I could have ever imagined.

Chapter Seven — Xander

My first thought when we entered the bedroom was that I could think of Rhiannon while I performed this necessary duty. But seeing Thea timidly sitting on the bed touched something inside me. And as I removed her veil and looked into her soft, fearful eyes, I realized that it's not just me that has to bear this burden. From that moment on, I approached her with care. This wasn't going to be easy for either of us.

But how surprising it is to kiss her, to enter her and feel her tighten around me. As I thrust deeper inside her, my body responding to hers, I find myself only thinking of her and this moment between us.

As I get close, her soft moans fill my ears. I continue to move inside her. I can't describe how good she feels. Like nothing I've ever experienced. My wolf awakens inside me and threatens to burst forward and ravage her completely. It's taking everything I have to hold back. I don't know if she can withstand my full power.

I turn my head away. Looking at her, her hair loosened and flared out on the bed, her brow furrowing and her soft, pink lips slightly open with shaky moans. I can't... I must not...

She writhes under me, her legs shaking against me. I thrust harder, and her nails dig into my skin. The tendrils of pain mix with pleasure, nearly bringing my wolf to the surface. My claws come out and tear into the sheets.

Her back arches, and we both come together. I dare a look down at her to see her eyes glowing like golden sunlight. A long, loud moan escapes her as she comes. She shuts her eyes as it passes, and when she opens them again, the glow is gone, returned to their original soft blue color.

The deed done, I roll off her, a part of me regretting the separation. I'm lying on my back next to her, the both of us struggling to regain our breaths. As we lie here, the sounds of howling in the distance spills in through the open window. She jerks up, looking around with wide eyes.

"It's the full moon tonight," I remind her. "Many are rising to bask in its effects."

She doesn't say anything for a moment, then, "It isn't affecting you?"

"It is," I say softly. "I'm holding myself back."

She nods her head and slowly lays back down. We lie there, listening to the echo of howls in the night as we stare at the ceiling.

She says in a quiet voice, "So when is it supposed to happen?"

Before I can answer her, she stops and gasps, cutting herself off. I look over to see her grimacing, her arms wrapped around her center. She starts screaming, rolling over onto her side and then onto the floor. I sit up slowly, watching as she writhes in pain.

It's starting.

I climb out of the bed and stand a little ways from her, keeping watch in case she loses control, which she might. I'm a little worried since I've never encountered a creature like her before. I'm a strong wolf, but she is something more than just a wolf. There is no guarantee that I can handle whatever it is that she is about to become. I only hope I am enough to keep her contained.

The room fills with the sound of her bones breaking one by one. She howls out in pain with every snap, and a part of me aches. To go through this the way she is, having never experienced the change. It's terrifying for us in the best of circumstances. I cannot imagine what it is for her.

The cracking of bones continues and so do her loud cries. Her claws spring out from her fingers, then her limbs twist back and change. Snow-colored fur spreads across her skin as she morphs from human to wolf.

Fully changed, she raises her head up and howls to the moon, her voice shaking the floor under my feet. Surely, other wolves nearby can sense it as I do. This vibration of power coming over me. I'm compelled to howl with her. In the distance, a chorus of wolves joins us.

The song dies away, and she turns to me, fixing her golden eyes on mine. A low growl emanates from her as she takes a step back from me. Her wolf is new like a whelp just experiencing the world. I kneel down before her and extend my hand to her. Her growl subsides, the human memory mixing with her wolf instinct to tell her who I am.

I shift, turning into my animal. She shrinks back as I do so quickly, but once I am a wolf, she relaxes, understanding coming over her.

I reach out to her, mind-linking to connect with her. Her mind is just noise. Animal and human sounds mixing as they fight for control. *Shhh*, I say to her. *Focus on my voice.*

She blinks her gold eyes at me, then, *Are . . . are you talking to me?*

Yes. As wolves, we can communicate this way.

There's another rash of words and sounds, images. I flinch a little. The information she's sending me is slightly overwhelming. *Try to pull back your thoughts.*

After a moment, the noise subsides. I tell her, *Now, think in words to me. Speak as if you are using your mouth.*

Silence, then, *Like . . . like this?*

Yes. That's it. You've got it.

This is . . . strange, she says. *Can I do this all the time?*

We can only do this as wolves. It helps us work together in battle.

Nothing for a moment, then, *That's its only use?*

I don't know how to answer that. It's the only way I've ever used it, after all.

She begins to whimper suddenly, shrinking away from me. Her body starting to shiver from the urge to shift back to human. I shift back to human as she changes, her bones snapping back into place again.

She is human, naked, lying on the floor before me and shaking like a leaf. I step forward to help her, but she manages to get up to her knees. She goes to stand but swoons a little. Then her head and shoulders fall back, her golden eyes now staring at the ceiling.

She stands before me, swaying slightly from side to side, her mouth moving and soft words coming out. I don't understand what she's saying. "Thea?"

Upon hearing her name, she stops and lowers her head, locking me into her golden gaze.

Then she inhales a long breath and falls forward. I catch her in my arms. As I look down at her, she closes her eyes. She's passed out.

Early this morning, one of the elders stopped by my room, curious to know how things went. I sent him away. I need more time with Thea before they can weigh in. This all must be handled delicately.

After all, it's sealed now. She's the actual hero for us all. The one we have been waiting for all this time. My doubts have been tempered.

While she slept, I cleaned up and dressed myself. There is a lot that needs to be done before she can be reintroduced as my mate.

My mate. My *Luna*. I don't think I'll ever get used to that. I go over to the window and look down on the courtyard and beyond the fortress to the town around us. I find myself wondering if, now that her powers have manifested, an exception can be made for me. Wolves mate for life, and normally, it would not be a discussion. But I did not choose her, and she did not choose me—fated or not, we are not supposed to be together.

When all this is over, I want to get back to Rhiannon and the life I'd planned. I will have to appeal to the elders, but surely I can make them see sense.

I hear Thea stir and I turn around. She sits up in bed, rubbing sleepy eyes. She looks remarkably sexy, with her whitish-blonde morning hair all over the place and falling over her delicate shoulders.

The sheets have slipped down to her waist, her full and perfect breasts on display. My eyes drop down to them, the memory of how they felt in my hands coming back to me.

She sees me looking and quickly grabs the sheets to cover herself. I force down the smile that wants to form on my lips, and I go to my closet to find my training gear.

"Good morning," she says in a raspy voice.

"Mm," I grunt.

She stays quiet, but I can feel her heated gaze on my back. I hope she's not thinking there is anything more to last night than sex. I don't want to have to remind her that this was all just duty.

"Um. How did last night go?" she asks.

The sex or the change? "You don't remember?"

She shakes her head, then says, "Well . . . the sex, I remember. The rest is kind of hazy."

I take that in. I guess such a traumatic experience may have that effect. "As expected," I answer, though that's probably the furthest thing from the truth. I didn't expect a lot of what happened last night. And not just with her change as a Daywolf. I'm still mulling over the fact that I was able to orgasm to *her* alone and the lingering feelings around that.

"Why do you hate me?" she asks out of the blue.

My fingers halt on the belts around my waist. She continues.

"Since you found me, you've been nothing but mean to me. The first act of kindness you even showed me was last night when we . . ." She trails off. Then, "I don't get why. What have I done to make you so angry with me?" I just scoff. She sighs and says, "So, then, you're not even going to tell me? Don't you think that's kind of childish?"

"If you understood anything about your situation, you'd watch your foolish tongue around me."

She doesn't respond and for a moment, I think that I've shut her up. But then, she says, "You're the only one who looks down on me and I'm supposed to be the 'Chosen One'. Don't I have a right to know why that pisses you off?" I tilt my head and turn to face her. "I'm sorry," I say. "Are you expecting me to fall all over your feet thanking you for your existence, or do you somehow think that because of last night, we're now supposed to fall in love and live in paradise? You are childish and unworthy of me. I am the Alpha. This is my pack, and everything I do is for them." I gesture at the bed. "Including all of this. Last night, I was kind to you because it was the decent thing to do. Don't mistake that for love. Are we clear?"

She just stares at me with watery blue eyes. Then she nods quickly.

"Good. Get dressed. You're due for your training."

I turn and finish putting on my gear, then I leave without looking back. The hurt look on her face is burned into my mind. It had to be said, though. There should be no illusions between us.

It's better she knows now that this is an arrangement and that's all it will ever be. She's not entitled to anything just because everyone else regards her with reverence.

"Is that a hickey?"

My eyes shoot up at Conan, who's leaning into me and pulling at my collar. I shove him away from me, and he bursts into laughter.

We're standing outside in the training circle, going over a few drills with Akila and Branson. Conan's messing with me, of course, which is making it difficult to concentrate.

"How's she feeling?" Akila asks. "We all felt and heard her change last night."

"I'll say," Conan interrupted. "Felt like I could leap a canyon after she howled. You must have really given it to her, Big Dog." He nudges me, and I slap his hand away.

"I will toss you on your ass, Conan."

"You will try."

"Honestly, Conan," Akila interjects, "you know he didn't do it for pleasure, right? This was to save us all."

"Exactly," I chime in. "And if it's all the same to you, I'd like to focus on our training. Especially since she'll be joining us in a bit."

Silence from all of them. As they all exchange glances with one another, I sigh, thoroughly done with their bullshit. "What?"

"What about Rhiannon?" Akila asks. "I mean, she's going to be out here any second and—"

"She'll have to adjust," I say. "As will we all. There's nothing to be done for the situation, and she knows that."

I don't like how the mood has changed around me. They all seem like they know something I don't. Like

Rhiannon is suddenly going to explode the second she sees Thea. I know she's not happy about the situation, but I also know she wouldn't go against my or the elders' wishes.

As if summoned, Rhiannon appears on the training field. She walks right past me and over to Akila like I'm not even here.

"Ready to do this?"

"Yeah," Akila answers. "We'd better get on with this. Alpha?"

Rhiannon doesn't really look at me. Like everyone, she felt Thea's pull last night. I can't imagine how unpleasant that must have been for her.

But now isn't the time to talk about it. We've got work to do. I sort everyone in their places, separated by skill level for effectiveness. Some are in their human form, looking to practice speed, while others have already summoned their wolves to practice their strength and agility.

"Akila," I say, "I want you leading this team. Rhiannon—"

"Holy shit," Conan says, adding a whistle.

I turn to see Thea walking out and toward us. She's dressed in her training gear—a leather belt and sash like mine and fingerless leather gloves, fit for claws. Her long blonde hair is tied back and away from her face and her blue eyes look determined, even though her soft, feminine features are betraying her. She still looks to me like a silly child playing dress up.

Everyone has stopped whatever they were doing to stare at her, watching intently as she walks up to us all. She's looking around nervously, doing her best not to meet anyone's eyes, her arms stiffly at her waist.

Akila steps forward, stopping before her and saying, "Welcome to training. You'll be with me."

She nods and smiles delicately, clearly thankful for Akila's olive branch. I look away, denying myself the pleasure of her smile.

"All right, then," I say, turning to them all. "It's wolves and humans. We'll try grappling first, then move on from there. Akila, do you need a moment with your team?"

She looks over at Thea, then back to me. "If I can be paired with Thea—"

"No. She'll have to learn on her own. Just as we did. Let's begin."

I'm not sure what to expect by throwing her in this way, but I figure that if she's really as powerful as they say, then this will be old hat.

A couple of wolves manage to pin her without much effort. Into the dust she goes, again . . . and again. She gets back up every time, though. I can't help but watch as she makes mistake after mistake and ends up with her back against the ground.

Still, she gets up. I've lost count now of how many times she's been felled.

So little skill and so much heart. It's interesting to watch.

She's getting more aggravated with every slam into the dirt and now it's irritating me. I'm beginning to hate watching this. Frustration for her sake, perhaps? I can't imagine how hard this must be for her.

I let them regroup after the last round, and Akila jogs over to give her encouragement. I turn my head for a moment, and the next thing I know, I hear a growl and a yell. I turn to see Rhiannon as a wolf, pinning Thea to the ground. Rhiannon is baring her teeth and snarling while Thea grabs her by the throat to hold her off.

"Hey!" Akila shouts, "Rhiannon, stop!"

I run over, lowering myself and shoving a shoulder into Rhiannon to get her off. Rhiannon rolls off and shifts to human. She crouches in the dust, glaring up at me angrily.

"I was not finished," she snarled. "*We* are not finished."

"Rhiannon—"

"Is she to learn anything at all? Why do you coddle her?! You will not be able to save her in a real battle--"

"You are out of order," I say in a firm tone. "Wait until the next round."

Rhiannon says nothing. She just stands up and dusts her naked form off, then shifts back into a wolf and goes back to her team.

I look back at Thea to see Akila helping her to her feet. A pang of anger and guilt emanates from my center. I can sense Thea's feelings, something I've heard mated pairs are able to do. She's not angry. Frustrated, yes, but there's no malice within her for the attack. She's even chuckling a little.

"Keep your composure," I tell everyone else as I walk back to my place. "Losing your head in battle could literally mean losing your head. Remember, we are animals, but we are not beasts. Get ready to go again."

We move on. I do my best to ignore what I'm feeling from Thea. The hit from Rhiannon was deliberate and, well, expected. Yet, it has done nothing to break Thea's spirit. In fact, she seems to be learning. Adjusting. She's still on her back more than on her feet, but she's getting it. I will never admit this, but I think I'm starting to feel pride for the determination she's expressing.

Mother comes out and watches the training with me for a moment. She stands just outside the ring, her white robes not daring to touch the dirt. "She still has a lot to learn," she says.

"Yes. But she's getting the hang of it."

She nods slowly. Then, "There is hope for us yet, my son."

I take a deep breath. I certainly hope she's right.

Chapter Eight — Thea

We've trained for most of the day, and I'm still sore from it, even after a long bath in the solitude of Xander's bathroom. I guess I should think of it as my bathroom as well, being that he's my mate or husband or whatever now.

It's dinnertime, which is . . . well, oddly enough, everything I'd expect from this influential wolf pack family. There are dining rooms in the fortress, but tonight, we're sitting at a long wooden table under the stars in the courtyard, and there's a feast before me that looks like something out of a medieval fairy tale. Large silver platters of fruit and vegetables, well-cooked birds and roasts, and it all smells so good.

My understanding is that Gemma, my new mother-in-law, has decided to celebrate our nuptials, and that's why there are so many people here. I see a few faces that I've only been vaguely acquainted with before. I guess tonight is the night to get to know everyone.

But I think I might've already fucked up a little. When I walked in, I was directed to sit next to my "husband," who took the head of the table with his mother at his left side. I was told to sit on the right. I chose another seat about four away, yielding to Rhiannon, who gladly took the seat next to him. I noticed glances of disapproval, but no one said anything, including the so-called "Alpha."

Gemma stands, interrupting the conversation around us. She raises a glass. "A toast. To the continuous peace and harmony in our pack." She looks at me with her gentle smile. "And to Thea."

Everyone agrees with a hearty "Hear, hear." I glance over at Xander, who's not even meeting my gaze. What a terrible marriage this is turning out to be.

"Don't worry," I hear next to me. Xander's brother, Luther, took the seat next to me and is now leaning over in my ear. "He will grow to love you eventually . . . or maybe he won't. It wasn't exactly a requirement, was it?"

I pick up my fork and dig in. I should at least look like I'm hungry, even though my stomach is in knots. "You can keep your opinions to yourself," I say in a low voice to Luther. "This whole thing is hard enough without peanut gallery comments."

He shrugs. "Sorry if it offends you, but you did choose this course all on your own."

"I don't see where I had a choice."

"My dear sister-in-law," he says with a snicker, "you must learn that there is one fundamental truth about life. You *always* have a choice, even if the choice is undesired."

I don't respond to that. He might be right, but it's kind of a shitty move to bring it up now.

I glance back over at Xander, who's looking my way. He looks pissed. But then, he always kind of looks pissed. I don't think he likes his brother next to me, though. The way he's watching us reminds me of the day in the courtyard when Luther came up to chat. Clearly, there's something here that I'm missing.

"Oh, look at the time," Luther says suddenly. He finishes his wine in one gulp and wipes his face with a napkin. "As much as I would love to stay here with you to continue our chat, there is a situation that needs my immediate attention. If you would excuse me."

"Sure," I reply. Without another word to anyone, he stands and leaves the dinner table.

Did I enjoy his conversation? No.

Am I glad that he's leaving? Maybe.

Will I smile and feign attention to him because I know it might piss Xander off? *Hell, yes.*

"So, Thea," Akila says, her eyes lighting up in the amber light around us. "How are you feeling? I know it was a hard day for you at training."

I shrug a little, but I smile. As awful as the training was, I actually enjoyed it for the most part. It was refreshing to get some of this frustration out. "I'm sore," I say to her. "But I'm okay."

"That'll pass. Trust me."

"You kicked ass, though," I say, eager to keep up the conversation.

"You mean I kicked *your* ass," she says with a raise of her eyebrows. I laugh.

"Yeah. I guess you did."

"It's your first training, though," she says with a smile. "You'll definitely get better with time and more practice."

God. I hope so.

"She'd better get better if she's going to survive around here." It was Rhiannon who just spoke. She smiles over at me and says, "If you can't even take a wolf of my size, I expect you'd be destroyed in a real fight."

"I'll get better," I say, sitting up a little. "Just give me a little time."

"Right. Because time is the one thing we've got tons of."

"That's enough, Rhiannon," Xander says. Rhiannon gives him a momentary look of hurt, then looks back at me. She doesn't apologize or even take any of her snark back. She just looks down at her plate like she's been slapped on the nose with a newspaper.

"Would you be interested in knowing some of the history of this pack?" Gemma chimed in. "Akila, Conan, Branson, and Rhiannon were all born during the same whelping season."

Not sure what she means by whelping, but I get the gist. "So, you all grew up together?"

All but Rhiannon nodded in response. She was quietly pushing the food around on her plate. "We've all been close," says Akila. "Especially Conan and . . ." She trails off, her face blanching as she glances over at Xander. After a second of awkwardness, she clears her throat and adds, "We've always been a particularly close-knit pack."

"Some of us a little too close," I hear Conan mutter. Akila kicks him under the table.

"Anyway," she says, pulling focus back to her. "I can imagine how hard it is to be introduced to a pack like ours. You must feel like more of an outsider than you are."

"It most certainly doesn't have to be that way," Gemma says. "The camaraderie that you all learned as whelps, you can pass on to Thea now that she's one of us."

Akila nods. "If you like, I can give you some pointers during the off hours if you want."

I smile at Akila. She's probably the only person here who's been nice to me without an agenda. "I'd like that very much, thank you."

"I think I've had enough," Rhiannon says, pushing her plate away. "If you all will excuse me, I'm going to turn in." She looks to Xander and Gemma in turn. "Good night, my Lord, Madam."

She turns and leaves. Xander looks after her, a sort of sorrow on his face. He's been such an ass to me during this whole thing, and so has Rhiannon, but I feel terrible for them both. None of us asked for this situation, after all.

My hand clutches my glass of wine, and I lift it to my lips and down it in one go. Rhiannon's gone, but Xander still looks pensive. Asshole that he is, I guess this whole thing kind of sucks for him, too. I wish I could offer some kind of comfort to him. Not that he'd take it if I was so bold as to do so. He'd slap away any kindness I showed him.

Dinner goes on. Once it's done, I thank Gemma for the food and wish her a good night, then I leave without saying a word to my "husband." I'll be sleeping in the room I was in before last night from here on out. There's no point in pretending that we're together... especially when it's not me that Xander really wants.

It's been two nights, and we've slept apart without incident. We don't even really spend any time together otherwise. When we see each other in the hallways or the courtyard, all that's exchanged are glances between us. Never any words.

I wish it were as easy as being away from him, though. Xander has stayed away from me, but that hasn't stopped me from feeling him. I can sense him when he's near now, almost all the time. Sometimes, it's just a feeling, but most of the time, I can hear his heartbeat and pick up his sweet and woody scent. There have been moments when I was walking down one of the halls, and I knew he was coming before he even rounded the corner.

And... and he stands by my door at night. At least he has for the last two nights, anyway. He never knocks or makes himself known audibly, but I can feel him there. Standing guard, perhaps. It's like he wants to be sure I'm inside and asleep before he goes to bed himself.

Maybe it's the familiarity of knowing he's there, but I'm starting to like the way he smells. It's a strange, airy scent. Like the woods, but with a subtle hint of wildflowers.

At night, I lie in bed and I think about what I left behind. Sometimes, I wonder how far I'd actually get if I tried to leave. That's the worst thing about all this. I wouldn't even know what direction to run if I did try to take off. I don't want to be here, but I don't see any way out of here. Sometimes, I can see the walled borders from my window at night, and I wonder if I could get beyond them and what I would find. Would there be someone out there who could help me get back home?

Would they even *know* what home was for me? I'm in a place where werewolves are real. Where I'm apparently, part werewolf. It just isn't fair. I wish they'd just left me alone.

But here we are, early in the morning, for training. Like she promised, Akila has been stopping by in the evenings to show me a few things I can use during training. I think it's helping some, and I seem to be learning more and more about my powers and how to control and use them.

As I walk out to meet the group, Akila runs up to me, a big smile on her face.

"We're switching it up today," she says.

"Okay. What do you mean?"

"So, you've been training your human form the last couple of days, and that's fine and everything, but we've decided that it's time for us to see what your animal can do."

I instantly become nervous.

"Wait," I say, looking at everyone else warming up behind her. "You . . . you want me to change into a wolf. Out here?"

She nods. "Yeah. We'll see how well you can move and attack and—hey, you okay?"

I must look like I'm going to throw up. I certainly feel like I might. "I . . . I've only changed once. And I didn't have any control over it . . . and won't I be naked? I don't know about this." I'm starting to ramble. Akila takes me by the shoulders.

"First of all, don't be ashamed of being naked. No one cares. I don't know if you've noticed, but people are naked all the time around here. It's not a big deal. And secondly, you need to do this eventually. You're going to need to explore the full range of your powers."

I bite my lip and shift my foot from one side to the other. She smiles comfortingly. "Don't worry. You're among friends."

I have vague memories of changing on my wedding night. I don't know how I did it then or how to even do it again if I can. And while my memory's hazy on it, I do remember it hurting like a bitch. When everybody else does it, it's easy and painless. I'm nowhere near that yet.

But looking at Akila, she seems to think I can do this. And if I don't trust anyone here, I trust her. I return her smile and say, "Okay."

Just then, Xander arrives, walking past us as if we're not here. "All right," he says loudly, and everyone stops what they're doing to pay attention. "We're pairing up in wolf form today." He looks over to Akila, "You've explained it to her?"

She nods. Xander looks at me. "Good. I'm pairing you with Rhiannon today."

Both Akila and I exchange glances, and Akila, reading the instant look of fear on my face, speaks up. "Is that the best idea? Given everything that's happened—"

"She's one of the best soldiers in our pack," he says simply and without malice or anger. "Thea must be at the top of her game. Rhiannon has been told to keep herself in check already. I don't expect she will be foolish enough to disobey me."

Rhiannon is standing a little off to the side and, upon hearing her name, takes a step forward and says, "I'm ready, my Lord."

"Good. Change, and let's begin."

I wished I'd been told before now, although I don't know what good it would have done me. I turn to Rhiannon, who immediately changes without a second thought, her body shifting and changing before me. Her clothes fall from her body as she walks out of them, shaking her head to brush them off.

Showoff.

I look away and close my eyes, trying to summon up that feeling I had when I shifted before. Nothing happens at first. I hear Akila whisper, "Just put it all out of your mind. The wolf is already inside you. When you call for it, it'll come."

I nod. Then I inhale and exhale slowly, thinking of the wolf and visualizing me calling for it. In another second, my bones start to crack painfully. I grit my teeth and bear it, letting it take over and change me from the inside out. It takes nearly a minute, but before I know it, I'm on all fours, claws in the dirt, fur covering my bare skin.

In the next second, I'm knocked down. Rhiannon has charged toward me and head-butted me with a force that sends stars to my eyes. I shake it off and get to my feet, bracing myself for another impact. She charges me again, but I sidestep her once, twice. She catches me on the third time, swiping at me with her claws and snapping at me. I back up a few steps, and when she charges again, I sidestep her, throwing my body into her right flank.

She stumbles, then whirls around, baring her teeth and growling angrily. *Mine . . .*

I hear her just as clearly as if she'd said it aloud. I freeze in surprise, and she takes that moment to leap at me. I manage to dodge, but I don't get all the way out of her way. She slams into my hips and knocks me to the ground. A sharp pain jolts through my right leg.

I look down to see Rhiannon has wrapped her canines tightly around my leg. I howl and try to pull my leg away, but she's got a grip on me, digging her teeth in and holding me down.

Panic sets in and I change. The cracking of my bones is nothing compared to the pain in my leg right now. As soon as I'm human again, she releases me and pounces, her paws digging into my shoulders as she presses me into the ground. I grab her neck, and my claws pop out, digging into her fur as she snaps at my face. I press my thumbs into her throat, and she gags, pulling away long enough for me to kick her off me. As she gets to her feet, I leap at her, grabbing her by the neck and picking her up. She squirms under my grip, her tongue hanging out as I choke the light out of her.

Seeing her like this, something snaps inside me. I'm filled with a warm, radiating power and I feel stronger than I ever have. I can actually see myself crushing her windpipe with ease. It wouldn't even take but a flinch of my fingers.

And in the next moment, my senses return and I realize how close I've just come to taking her life. I throw her to the ground. She rolls, but she's not deterred. She starts to leap at me again.

Akila comes out of nowhere, her wolf form knocking Rhiannon back. The two of them tumble in a flurry of dust and growling.

"That is *enough!*"

The command echoes across the ring, and everyone freezes, including Akila and Rhiannon. I suddenly feel the pain in my leg, and my knees buckle. I collapse to the dirt as Xander comes running up to me. As I sit here, a pool of blood forms beneath me, his jacket draped over my shoulders.

"Hey, it's okay," he says in a soft tone. "You're okay. Don't move. Healers are on the way."

I hear the whispers around me. I look up to see everyone staring back at us. Well, mainly at me. They're all wide-eyed with fear.

"Why didn't you change back?" Xander bellows at Rhiannon. "Didn't you hear me calling you?"

Rhiannon has shifted back, and she looks terrified. Blood drips from her mouth, and blue eyes as big as saucers bounce back from me to him. "I tried," she says. "I swear to you I tried, but I couldn't. It was like something was keeping me from changing. I couldn't stop myself."

"Thea?" Akila's sharp voice breaks my attention from them. "Didn't you hear us telling you to stop? You could have really hurt her."

"*I* could have hurt *her*??" she balked, rubbing the purple bruises around her throat. "Are you serious?"

I don't know what to say. I just sit there staring at Xander, who towers angrily over Rhiannon. I shake my head and say softly, "I . . . I don't know what happened. I'm, I'm sorry." I look at Rhiannon and say a little louder, "I'm *sorry*."

"Save it," she spits at me. She stands up, and Xander reaches out to her. She snatches her arm away from him. Then, with a dirty look at me, she limps off.

Xander turns an angry gaze at me, but he doesn't say anything. Seconds later, the healers come, and they help me up and lead me away from the training field. I don't look back, but I feel Xander's eyes on me as I go.

He can have Rhiannon for all I care. Xander pitting me against her was clearly a mistake that almost cost us both. I won't forget that.

Chapter Nine — Xander

What a mess that was. I watch as Rhiannon storms off, a mix of emotions swirling within me. She should have let go. She was too rough . . .

But no one could have anticipated Thea's response. I shudder to think what might've happened if Akila hadn't stepped in.

Rhiannon is one of our best warriors. I thought by choosing her as an opponent, Thea could be challenged to express her powers properly without too much injury to a less experienced wolf. In a way, I was right. Rhiannon will be fine. I shudder to think what Thea would have done to a novice soldier.

Thea has been taken back to the infirmary and I decide to follow to oversee Thea's care. Now that the dust is settled, we'll need to discuss what happened. I have an intense need to make sure she's all right. I saw how shocked she was about her own display of power. And everyone saw how she struggled to change to her wolf initially, something that took the average teen less time to do. There's much we have to discuss about her development.

As I pass Rhiannon's room, I feel compelled to stop. I know she's in there. Injured or not, she wouldn't dare to go to the infirmary where I sent Thea. *Since I'm here...*

I open her door slowly to see her sitting on her bed. She's holding a cooling satchel to her bruised ribs, icy smoke emanating from the small white pouch that encircles her dark red and purple bruises. As the door opens, she looks up at me and exhales.

"What are you doing here?" she says, a bitter tone in her voice. "Aren't you supposed to be with your mate right now? Or have you not seen enough of my epic embarrassment today?"

"How are you feeling?" I ask as I walk all the way into the room.

"How do you think?" she snaps. I just regard her silently. She rolls her eyes and answers, "It hurts like crazy right now, but it will probably heal in a few hours. Nothing I haven't dealt with before."

"That's good."

I sit next to her, and we both stay silent. Sitting here like this reminds me a little of me and Thea on our wedding night. The terrible situation that we both find ourselves in.

"You know," she says, breaking the silence, "she almost really hurt me out there." She lifts her head to show me the ring of purple and red forming around her neck. "I really thought for a second that she wasn't going to stop. If Akila hadn't torn her away from me—"

"Her powers have not fully manifested. We do not know the full range of her abilities just yet, and neither does she. You can't hold that against her."

Rhiannon raises amused eyebrows.

"Well. That was fast." She chuckles. "It took years for you to come to the realization that *we* were more than friends. What's it been? A month since she arrived, and already you're taking her side?"

"Rhiannon—"

"She almost killed me today, Xander. And you're sitting here talking to me about being . . . *sympathetic* to her?"

"It's the truth. She is something we've never encountered before. If I had matched her with a lesser fighter—"

"So, I get to be the test subject?"

I glare at her in shock. "No. Of course not. Listen, I never would have let her—"

"But you almost did. And need I remind you that it wasn't you who came to my aid, Xander? It was Akila. She saved me. Not you. And I think I know why."

I frown deeply at her. "What are you talking about? Say what you really mean."

"What I really mean? Ugh." She stands up and tosses the satchel across the room before turning to me. "I may not be your mate, Xander, but I still know you. You have feelings for her. Or at least, you are starting to and don't want to say so. As much as I hate to say it, what I have feared from this is finally coming to pass. You are falling in love with her."

I just stare at her. Completely speechless. My silence speaks volumes, though, and I can see she knows it. She nods her head slowly, then says, "I'd like you to leave."

"Rhiannon."

"I need to rest." She lowers her eyes away from mine like a submissive. Like a subject of lower rank. "Please."

I don't have anything left to say to her. I stand and walk out of her room. In the hallway, I pause for a long moment, her words echoing through my mind.

You are falling in love with her.

Am I? No. This is just a product of the mating ritual. I resume my path to the infirmary. Then I stop myself. I want to see how Thea's doing, but . . . why? I want to say that it's because it's my duty, but I can't deny the concern I have for her well-being. I can rationalize it in whatever way I want to, but that's the core of this need to see her. Stupid bond.

I thought I had long understood how mating works when I was with Rhiannon. Now, I think it's safe to say that I never understood it at all. We never got to be mated after all.

I think of Thea all the time. At night, I feel her distress when she's having a bad dream. During the day, I feel her worry to impress us and her disorientation with living in this new world. I felt her adrenaline rush while she trained and her fear when Rhiannon turned and bit her leg. I am connected to her, and it is completely infuriating.

She has yet to come back to my room, and while I have not asked her to, I find myself at her door every night, waiting for her to fall asleep.

Waiting for her to invite me in.

Fuck.

This bond is messing with my mind.

I turn and walk away from the infirmary. I am in no state to face Thea right now. Not while I'm wrestling with these emotions.

"Xander. There you are!"

I turn to see my mother coming down the hallway. I wait for her as she walks up. "I heard about training today. How is Rhiannon doing?"

"She's fine. There are minor bruises on her side and neck, but she should be back on her feet in a matter of hours."

"Mm. That's good. And Thea? Have you checked on her?"

I say nothing. Mother sighs. "I asked the seers to come evaluate her while her leg heals."

"Okay. What have they found?"

"Well, they have come to the conclusion that you both need to form a stronger connection."

I scoff. "A stronger connection. That's a joke, right?"

She shakes her head. "They say you're not in sync."

"Of course, we're not in sync. Neither of us wanted to be mated—"

"And yet, here we are." She speaks softly but firmly. "Xander, the bond of mating with her serves as a way to bind her powers to her. The stronger your connection is, the more powerful she will become and the faster and better she actualizes her powers."

"What are you saying? I'm her trigger?"

"It's much deeper than that," she says. "Xander, I know how difficult this is, but you must find a way to build on your initial bond with her."

"How do I do that? We barely *like* each other."

She pats me on my back and smiles up at me with her gentle smile. "You will find a way. I believe in you."

She walks away, leaving me confused and uncertain. I do not doubt the seers, but . . . what else must I do? *You will find a way,* she said. All right. I suppose I must find a way.

The sound of Mother's footsteps are the only ones I hear as I stand in this hallway, my mind in turmoil. I loathe the idea of bonding with Thea.

"I do this for the pack," I whisper to myself as I start walking towards the infirmary. "This is for the pack."

When I get there, Olcan is standing next to her as she lies in bed. He's applying the last of several bandages to her wounds. He looks up at me and smiles.

"Lord," he says in greeting. "Your mother stated that you may pay a visit to check in."

I don't look at Thea. I don't even want to acknowledge her. "How is she?"

"She's sitting right here," she snarks. "You can speak directly to me. I am conscious."

Olcan's face reddens. He clears his throat as he secures the last bandage. "She will be fine. Mere flesh wounds, no broken bones."

"Good. She should be fit for training tomorrow morning—"

"Excuse me?" she interrupted. "I'm not going back out there."

I'm starting to get a headache from her insolence. My displeasure is clearly showing on my face and Olcan steps in. "If I may, Lord Xander—"

"You may not," I tell him. "Leave us alone to talk."

He gives me this tentative look, then pats Thea on the shoulder as if offering encouragement. "Of course, Lord," he says as he walks out of the room. As soon as he's gone, she rolls her eyes at me.

"I would really appreciate it if you didn't give me a hard time right now," she says. "I've got enough stressing me out."

"Your comfort is of little concern to me."

She scoffs. "Of course it is. So what the hell do you expect from me, Xander? Is the lesson tomorrow how to fight with a bad leg? I've got stitches, you know and if I rip any of them—"

"Enough of your prattling. I tire of your complaining and whining—"

"Complaining?! You want to hear complaining?! Oh, that's a good one." She sits up in her bed, her eyes blazing rage at me. "I've been dragged to this make-believe land against my will, made to marry the biggest asshole this side of Wonderland, and to top it all off, I've got to fight actual fucking werewolves for eight Goddamn hours every day. And, God help me, I've done it about as much grace as I could possibly do in a situation like this—"

"Grace—"

"I'm not finished," she says through clenched teeth. "Let's be crystal fucking clear. The *last* place in this entire world that I want to be is here right now. And if I could come up with a way to get back home, believe me, I would do it in a heartbeat if for no other reason than to *never* look at your smug face again."

I glare at her, rage swirling like a storm inside me. "Are you finished?"

She glares back, her jaw set and her eyes boring holes into me.

"Let *me* be just as clear about your little situation, then," I growl. "Your only value to me or to anyone in this pack is the unfortunate circumstances of your existence. If I thought it was the true solution to the curse that plagues this land, I would toss you out of that window with barely a thought. You are *nothing* to me, Thea."

She stiffened her chin and replied, "Is that why you stand outside my door every night? Because I don't mean anything to you?"

It was like she'd slapped me and I take a step toward her. I stop myself, staying my hand by closing it into a fist at my side. "Shut your mouth about things you don't know."

"I know you're full of shit," she says in a low growl. "And I know that my leg is fucked up, so you won't see me on the training grounds until it's healed." I laugh, but she goes on. "I'm serious. I'm tired of your ordering me around like I'm not the fucking savior of this whole outfit. From here on out, I will do whatever I fucking please."

"You will follow my orders."

She narrows her eyes at me. "Eat a dick, Xander. This big bad wolf routine is old as fuck and I'm done with—"

I'm on top of her, the wolf inside of me threatening to come out as I pin her to the bed. She pushes her hand against my face and a white-hot pain shoots through me. I yelp and she pushes me off the bed.

I'm stunned...shocked...one side of my face tingles angrily. My reward for losing my temper. The wolf inside me retreats. *What the fuck...?*

The door opens and Olcan returns. He looks tentatively at the both of us. "Lord? I heard yelling. Is everything--?"

"It's fine," I say. "Carry on." I turn and leave. The seers want me to bond with her. *With her??* They clearly do not know what they are asking of me.

Chapter Ten — Thea

I'm in the dark again.

I'm not bound to a slab this time, but there's the same dank smell around me. Like I'm in a basement or a cave. I look around, trying to let my eyes adjust to the darkness. I can make out shapes but...

An amber glow rises from the center of the room and I see him sitting with his back to me. I can't see his face, but his dark hair and defined back are a dead give away. I just stand here, waiting for him to move. He doesn't.

"...Xander?"

The sound of my voice echoes off stone walls and he starts, his head turning to the side. His hair is too long. Tendrils of it hang in his face, hiding his eyes from me.

"You were supposed to save us," he says softly. "Why didn't you save us?"

He's almost whispering it, but his voice still sounds wrong. "Never should have brought you here. You were supposed to be my salvation...not theirs."

I can hear my own breath, shaky and nervous as I approach him. "What are you talking—?"

He whirls around and stands up, hovering over me. The shadows play tricks on his face, taking his long hair and using it to darken the top half of his face. I take a half step back, but he reached out and grabs me, yanking me to him.

"They promised! *They promised!!!*

His hands are turning into claws, digging into my skin. Jagged, wolf teeth appear behind his curled lips. He snarls...then roars, the sound deafening, shaking me down to my bones.

I sit straight up, a scream hanging at the back of my throat. I'm no longer in the cave. I'm sitting up in my bed in this room that I suppose is mine now. A nightmare...a new one from the one I usually have. *Great.*

I just sit in the moonlit darkness, my hands shaking in my lap. I don't want to think about what this nightmare must mean. I used to blow off the other one. Thinking it was just one of those things from a late-night snack or something. But since *that* one came true...

I think back to our fight. Xander was so angry...he really meant to hurt me. Is that what the dream means? Will Xander actually try to...

No. That doesn't make sense. I'm valuable to him. The whole town believes that. And even though he hates it, he believes it too. And even though he lost his temper with me, I was able to defend myself. I'm not sure he *could* hurt me if he really wanted to.

I take a deep breath and calm myself. It was just a dream. In fact, this one was probably nothing. My anxiety from being trapped here in Werewolf Bridgerton. I look out of my window and see the beautiful evening sky. There have to be a million stars...

I start to think of back home. I don't have any connection to my foster family anymore. Ethan was my only friend...my only family. He must be crazy with worry about me. I don't like to think about the fact that I probably won't see him again after this. This really might be the rest of my life...

I hear a heartbeat just outside my door. Without even thinking about it, I know it's him. Always out there listening. Waiting. I would have thought that he'd avoid me like the plague after our fight earlier...

Guess not. Maybe he's come to apologize. I bite my lip and debate it for a moment. Then I make a decision. No sense in him standing out there in the hall.

Chapter Eleven — Xander

I felt her terror. It woke me from my own sleep as if I had been shaken. Before I was even fully awake, I left my room and rushed to hers. Ready to defend...

...what? I'm standing here just outside her door, listening to her heartbeat slow and feeling her anxiety fade. She had a bad dream. Of course. No one would be foolish enough to attack her here.

I should go back to bed. But...I can't. I just stand here, listening to her, *feeling* her. I don't fully understand why I'm compelled to be here, especially after our fight and even after talking to Mother and Rhiannon.

I don't know how to do this. I have to admit that to myself. She infuriates me and yet, I am drawn to her in a way I've never been drawn to anyone. My natural inclination is turning to her and…I don't really understand it. Worst of all, the guilt from attacking her has been weighing on me. My face still tingles a little from where she pushed me. At least now I know she's not nearly as weak as I thought she was.

Her breaths have softened. It's almost as quiet as cream beyond this door. She's probably asleep. I should return to my room now. This urge to be around her…I can meditate on it in the morning. There's no need to disturb her. . I turn to leave.

"Are you going to keep lurking at my door every night?" Her voice echoes clearly through the door.

I take the implied invitation and open her door. She's sitting on her bed and wearing a sheer nightgown, her leg wrapped securely in bandages.

"I do not lurk."

She scoffs but says nothing to that. "How is Rhiannon? You never mentioned how she was doing."

"Healing. She's tough. She'll be okay by the morning."

She nods in response and doesn't say anything for a moment. I feel the worry swirling up from her. Or maybe it's fear. She has every right to fear me after my behavior this afternoon. She pauses, opening her mouth to speak, then closes it, rethinking what she means to say.

"You should know," she says softly, "that it was not my intention to hurt her. I just . . . panicked, I guess. All I could think about was getting away from her and . . . I don't know. Everything else is kind of hazy after that. I was acting on autopilot or something."

Standing this close to her, after everything has calmed down, I feel real concern for Rhiannon, for Thea. I can see that she truly didn't mean for any of it to happen.

"Rhiannon is a soldier," I say in an effort to reassure her. "That is the sort of thing she has been training for."

Thea regards me silently, then looks away. Taking that in.

"It must be hard making decisions like that, being a pack leader and all."

"It is . . . challenging, to say the least. Nothing could have truly prepared me for the decisions I must make for this pack."

"I'll bet," she says with a little smile. "Akila told me that you became Alpha at a very early age."

"Yes. My father died when I was twelve. So I had to learn to lead and all it entails quickly."

My mother's words come back to me, and I realize this is the opportunity that I need to bond with Thea. But first...first, we must discuss my behavior. I point to the chair next to the bed. "May I?"

She nods. I take a seat and say, "I want to apologize to you...for earlier. I lost my temper in a way that was unbecoming of me. I'm sorry."

She's just staring at me as if waiting for more. Finally, she says, "Apology accepted. I shouldn't have told you to eat a dick."

I laugh and to my surprise, she laughs with me. "I guess we both lost our heads a little."

"Don't think I'm letting you entirely off the hook," she says. "You can't go around jumping on people who piss you off, werewolf or not."

"I understand...and I know. One of the first things I was ever taught was that we are civilized creatures. We are not beasts. How I behaved was shameful."

"Agreed," she says, though the anger in her eyes is gone. She reached out and touched my hand. It was warm and inviting. "How was it growing up without your father to lead you?"

That gives me pause. I'm not expecting her to reach out to me like this and my first reaction is to recoil...I resist, however. She's only asked a question. I should answer her. "Well," I begin. "For one thing, I am different from many other Alphas in Clarion in that I am of royal birth. My cousin is the current Alpha King, you see. He rules all of Clarion while lesser Alphas rule certain regions. Most of them have their positions by challenge or circumstance. But not me. My place here had to be decided by the Moon Goddess, even though becoming Alpha is technically my birthright."

"Wow," she says. "So, someone else could have become Alpha in your place?"

I nod. "And it wouldn't have taken much either since I was so young. My mother realized that and made sure that I was trained rigorously by the time I came of age. I was put through strict tests of my strengths and weaknesses. Both physical and psychological."

"That couldn't have been easy."

"It would have been worse if I was challenged. Fortunately for me, I wasn't."

She nods. "Your father . . . how did he die?"

I don't say anything at first. Speaking of my father's death . . . it's still fresh in my mind, even after all these years, and it probably will be forever. I rarely speak of it.

"You don't have to say anything if you don't feel comfortable talking about it," Thea says when I don't answer. I almost take her at that, but a stronger bond . . .

"My father," I begin, "and a few other elders and soldiers had gone away to negotiate a peace treaty of sorts. It was supposed to end the feud we had with another wolf pack. We had high hopes for it. The feud had been going on for a few generations at that point. On their way back, they were ambushed."

I have to pause. The events of the day come back to me in full color. "I was playing with my friends like any other whelp might be. As we were about to come in to eat, there was a commotion at our gates. My father's party had returned . . . Only three of the ten that left were on their feet. My father was among the fallen."

"Oh, my God," she says softly.

"I still remember how he looked. The way they carried him in, his face covered in blood . . . I didn't even realize it was him until I saw our family's sigil on his collar." I pause again, forcing the sorrow back down before it manifests itself in tears. I take a deep breath and finish. "He lived only a few hours, just long enough to tell my brother and I to take care of our mother, and to continue to lead and serve those who put their safety and trust in us."

"I am so sorry," Thea says. I shake my head and wave her off.

"He died for his pack. Something that every leader expects and is honored to do. There is no greater reward than knowing that in your last breaths, you lived to serve your people."

"He sounded like a good father." Her voice is now distant, and I look at her.

"Yeah, he was the best."

She squeezes my hand, and to my surprise, I don't pull away from her. That feeling of recoiling is gone. "You've really taken his words to heart with all this, then."

I nod. "Of course. You are what's good for this pack. I have to honor that."

She sits up a little taller, and I think I see a little smile on her face. "I ought to learn from you, I guess. You have something bigger than yourself to believe in. That's kind of hard for me."

"Oh, I don't know," I say, returning her smile. "All things considered, you've settled in nicely here. I imagine the rest will come with time."

She releases a nervous chuckle. "Yeah, I don't know about that. I am obviously still trying to figure this whole thing out." She holds out her wounded leg.

"Yes, well, injuries notwithstanding, I'd say you were doing well."

She gives a wan smile and pulls her hand back. I can feel her withdrawing from me suddenly. "Thanks for the lip service," she says, "but I'm not a fool. I know this isn't exactly the smoothest of transitions. For any of us."

"I guess you're right in that," I say to her. "But as it stands, we only have one another now. Truly. Regardless of how it happened, we...need one another."

Her eyes widen slowly, crystal blue in the amber light of the room. She smiles at me, tilting her head a little. "Spoken like a true leader."

That connection Mother spoke of, I feel it now. I can feel myself getting drawn into her gaze. She is a force, and she will soon realize that by herself.

I pull myself out of her gaze and stand. "I should take my leave," I tell her. "It's late, and you should rest that leg if you mean to walk on it again."

"Yes, my Lord," she says with a little laugh. I stand over her as she looks up at me, her smile fading slightly as our eyes lock. I listen to her heart pounding as we stare, some unspoken vibration between us. The urge to touch her face the way I did on our wedding night is almost more than I can bear.

I resist, however. That's enough bonding for tonight, I think.

"Goodnight, Thea."

"Goodnight." She replies in a breathy voice.

I leave. The second I'm on the other side of the door, I desperately wish I had not left at all.

Chapter Twelve — Thea

It's been an interesting bunch of days since the night I invited Xander into my room. A few times, Akila has caught me smiling like an idiot whenever he came near or staring at him longingly. I can't deny it. I'm definitely getting more into this whole mating thing with Xander.

At some point, Xander explained how it's important for us to "bond" because it'll help strengthen my powers. I think he might've been skeptical at first, but it seems like it's working out. We spend nearly every day together now, and I'm enjoying every second of it. If I don't see him during the day, no matter the reason, he's at my door every night before I go to bed. We sit on my bed and catch up with the events of the day.

It's gotten so that I actually want him to kiss me again. Since our first night together, he hasn't made a single attempt to kiss me or do anything sexual with me. It's not like I'm horny all the time, but whenever he's around, I always have to fight the urge not to grab him and plaster my mouth on his.

All this is so weird. Not that long ago I was ready to jump over the wall and take my chances on the outside. Now...now I'm wondering if I had been too hasty before. My nightmares are still making an appearance every so often, but when I wake up, Xander is there to hold my hand.

During training today, I did much better than usual, though Conan spent equal time joking and tossing me around like a rag doll. Still, by the time we were done, he helped me off the ground and patted me on the back. "Way to go, Thea," he said. "You're almost there."

I never thought I'd say this, but it's starting to feel like I belong here.

As night starts to fall, I'm sitting in the living room of Xander's quarters, watching as the sky starts to turn from bright to dark. The full moon is tonight, and I'm looking forward to it like a little girl in a candy store. I can sense the change in the air the closer the night comes. Like a sort of thrumming that touches me right to the core. Since I don't really remember what it was like on my wedding night, I'm eager to see how my powers manifest once the moon has risen.

They say the moon heightens our powers, and I can't wait to have the experience of changing under the full moon. I'm giddy in my shoes.

"Hey," Xander says as he walks into the living room.

"Hi." That I'm-so-horny feeling rushes into my body. Just the sound of his voice does it most days.

"Looking forward to tonight?" he says with a smile. My smile widens just looking at him. He doesn't smile nearly enough, and he should. His entire face lights up.

"How can you tell?" I say, crossing my arms smartly. He just chuckles.

"I can sense it from you."

"Oh." I forgot about that whole mated sense thing. I wonder if he can sense *everything* I'm feeling.

"What else can you sense from me?" I ask him with a playfully raised eyebrow. He looks at me for a long moment, then strides over to me, kneeling by my chair. He takes my hand, his fingers caressing the inside of my palm.

"The racing of your heartbeat," he says, the deep baritone of his voice sending chills up my spine.

"What else?" I whisper.

He stands and pulls me to standing, then leans into me, his hard body flush against mine. The heat from him mixes with my own, and his sweet, woody scent fills my senses. He trails a finger down my arm, and I bite my lip hard to keep my breath steady.

His mouth is dangerously close to mine as he says, "The heat of your body. Your sweet scent . . . especially when I'm near."

My face flushes, and all I want is to lean in and seal our lips together.

"Stay with me tonight," he says softly. I can't speak. I know he's asking more than just to have sex with him. He wants us to be together here as Alpha and Luna. I can sense that as much as I can feel his heart beating against mine. Him being this close to me is going to my head.

Footsteps sound behind him, breaking the moment. Two seers walk into the room, pausing as soon as they see us together. I immediately break away from him and take a step back.

Xander's eyes sharpen on mine for a moment. Then he looks over his shoulder at the two seers who have just walked into the living area.

"My Lord," one of them says, "your presence is requested in the meeting hall. Measures for this month's full moon are ready to be implemented."

"I'll be there in a moment."

They both nod and leave. He turns his silver-rimmed eyes to me and smiles gently. "I will be back after the moon has risen. Until then...will you wait for me here?"

I nod, still flushing, still wanting him desperately. He turns and leaves, and I watch him go.

I'll be waiting for him when the moon rises. Hell. I'll wait for him all night.

The full moon has risen, and a choir of wolf howls fill the night air all over Clarion. My body feels like it's on fire as I stand here, the moonlight casting down on me.

I'm resisting the urge to change. I want to wait for him to return. He said he would. God, I hope it's soon.

The door opens. The light from the windows cast shadows all around him as he walks in, his eyes on me lustfully.

I can feel all the wolves changing, their howls touching me with a million hands. My breathing has changed, and all I can think about is Xander. Xander's body with mine.

He walks over to me and takes me in his arms, touching my face delicately. The electricity from his hand courses through me.

"Is it always like this?" I whisper.

"Always. More for you because of what you are."

"I don't think I've ever felt like this before." I lean into him, my mouth searching for his. He pulls me into a kiss, his mouth eager and hungry. His hands move to the small of my back, and his claws prick me through my clothes. *Yes . . . rip my clothes off . . .*

He growls against my mouth, his fangs grazing my lip, sending a small slice of pain through me. My hands move down his chest, over his hard pecs, as I pull at the buttons of his shirt. I wince a little as claws push their way out of my fingertips.

I'm changing, and so is he. Wolves in passion on the night of a full moon. He picks me up suddenly and carries me to the couch, kissing my neck as his hands grab hold of my breasts. He's on top of me on the couch, his body between my legs. His rock hardness presses into me through his pants, rubbing against me through the all-too-thin fabric.

"I want you so bad," he says as his mouth moves down, claws threatening to tear my shirt right off my back.

The door suddenly flings open. A seer rushes in, his eyes wide and his face covered in sweat. "My Lord—" He stops, seeing us in our current state and averts his eyes. "I'm sorry to interrupt, but this is an emergency. We are under attack."

I watch as Xander's face changes to slate. He listens to the howls. We can both tell they are no longer joyful. There's distress in those cries.

He gets up, and we both walk over to the window. A wolf army has breached our gates, and a battle rages just under our window. I watch in horror, my feet suddenly glued to the floor. Members of our pack defend against the wolves, but it's not looking good. These wolves are bigger and so much more vicious.

I look around frantically at Xander, who's talking to the seer.

"Find my mother," he says. "Get her to the safe house."

"My Lord, what about you?"

"I will find the others and join the fight. Thea, go with him."

"What? N-no. I'm not going to leave you—"

"Now, Thea!"

I jump at the sound of his voice, but I obey him and start to follow the seer. Xander grabs me by the arm and kisses me hard before saying, "Stay safe, my love."

He pushes me away toward the door. The seer and I change to wolves, then run through the hallways to safety.

Hours have passed. I've spent most of it pacing and watching the doors. Xander went out there to fight with the rest of them. I don't know what's happened to him. What will I do if he's . . . if he . . .

He must be alive. I would feel it if he wasn't. Gemma and her attendants have been taking care of the children and the elders, I imagine, to keep her mind off the possibility of the worst. Why has this happened? Who would attack us?

Even though there are no windows here, I can sense the moon has set and dawn is now approaching. We don't know what we'll find when we leave here.

The doors open. Rhiannon, looking battered and bruised, walks in with several soldiers at her back. They immediately go to help the others. I rush over to Rhiannon.

"What happened? Is everyone— I mean, is Xander—"

"Calm down," she says and turns to Gemma. "Will you be all right? I need to escort Thea out of here."

"Yes, yes," Gemma says. "Go do your duty."

Rhiannon gives her a short nod, then leads me out of the safe house.

It's broad daylight, but the air is thick with gloom. Some of our pack members are carrying away the injured and dead, some treating their wounds on the spot. My heart is breaking for all this loss.

"Olcan is treating him," Rhiannon says as we move through the injured. She doesn't say anything more for a long time. Then, as if reading my mind, she adds, "You should know he fought bravely. He is responsible for saving a lot of lives today."

I nod and say nothing. My mouth is dry, and I'm on the verge of tears.

She leads me to the infirmary, and as soon as we walk in, the room is buzzing with activity. All the beds we can see are filled. Nurses and healers rush in and out.

"This way," Rhiannon says, guiding me to the room farthest down the hallway.

As soon as we open the door, I see him lying in bed, covered in bruises and bandages. His jaw and one of his eyes are swollen. Dr. Olcan stands over him, adjusting his IVs.

"How is he?" Rhiannon asks. Olcan looks over at us and sighs.

"He's taken a beating," he says. "But he'll be all right. I gave him a sedative to help him sleep while he heals. He'll need a few days of bed rest, but otherwise—"

"Oh, thank God," I say, walking across the room to his bed. I lean over him, brushing his hair out of his face. Every swelling and purple bruise makes me want to find who did this and rip them apart.

"I have matters to attend to, as I'm sure you do as well, Rhiannon?" Olcan looks to Rhiannon, who I notice is looking at us with a pained expression. She snaps out of it and nods to Olcan.

"There are more wounded coming," she says.

"Yes, I imagine there would be. Lead the way."

They leave, and now it's just the two of us here. I hold Xander's ice-cold hands, and I know by the touch how hurt he is. I pull up a chair by the bed and lay my head down on his chest, closing my eyes as I listen to his heartbeat. The rhythm eventually lulls me to sleep.

Three days have passed. I haven't left Xander's side. He hasn't awakened in all that time, but his bruises start to miraculously disappear. As I found out the day I was injured in training, wolves heal fast. For all my resistance, I could have returned to training the next day if I had wanted.

Gemma has been here and so have the members of his pack. Gemma was kind enough to bring me food and pillows to keep me comfortable. I thanked her, but all I care about right now is the moment that Xander opens his eyes.

It's almost noon, and my back hurts from sitting here for so long. Akila came in earlier to give me the news of the day, which is just that only a few of us were killed, despite the massacre I witnessed the morning after. Most survived, largely thanks to Xander. He really is the Alpha he strives to be.

"Thea?"

I look up to see his eyes fluttering open. He groans softly as he starts to wake, and I stand, excited. "Xander! Oh, thank heavens, you're okay."

I hug him, then I kiss his lips. He smiles against me, gently kissing me back.

"I was so scared when I first saw you in here," I say.

"I'm fine. I'm fine now," he reassures me.

Chapter Thirteen — Thea

This morning, Xander walked out of the infirmary like he was never hurt at all. He came back to our quarters with a healthy glow and the beginnings of a smile on his face the moment he saw me waiting for him in the living room.

He pauses, eyebrow raised, as he looks me over. "I woke up and you weren't in the infirmary."

I shake my head. "I rushed back here to tidy up for you. After everything you've been through, I didn't want you to see anything out of place. It's the last thing you need right now. I wanted to make sure you had a nice place to relax and rest up."

His smile widens a little. "I told you, Thea, I'm fine. Dr. Olcan even says so."

My face flushes a little. "I know. I'm just . . . I don't want . . . Well, what I mean to say—"

"Say it," he says, and my insides go all liquid.

"When you didn't wake up," I start, "I didn't know what to think. You looked so wounded and broken and I thought . . . I thought I'd lost you."

His eyes widen a little, and his smile drops. *Uh-oh. Too far?* I don't care. It was what I felt, and I'd be a damned fool not to say something.

"I...I decided to move back here with you. You...you're okay now, but I should be at your side. And I know this marriage isn't real, but—"

He closes the gap between us and wraps his arms around my waist, pulling me close to him. "I might have been wounded," he says, his voice vibrating between us, "but I cannot be broken."

My heart skips a beat as he looks deep into my eyes. This entire thing has been so strange. My feelings for him have gone from disgust to attraction to anger and now . . .

I want him. Desperately. Madly. Hearing his heartbeat in my soul, feeling his breath brush my face . . .

He leans in, and his lips connect with mine. We kiss, and I feel completely connected with him. Like he feels my need and that's all it takes to pull him into me.

He sweeps me up in his arms and carries me to the bedroom. He lays me down on the bed, his tongue and mine still intertwined as his hands move up my dress and along my bare thighs.

Here in this place, things like underwear aren't really a thing. It's taken a second to get used to wearing dresses and even my training gear without a pair of panties and a bra. I get it, though. After you've shifted a few times, I imagine the last thing you want to worry about is if your underwear is still on your furry body.

The other benefit, I'm finding, is in moments like this. As his hands move up and between my thighs, there's nothing keeping him from sliding his fingers between the wet folds of my sex. I gasp as his fingers find my clit, rubbing it slowly up and down.

The feeling sends warm shockwaves through me, and I grab hold of his hand. He's getting me there too fast. I'm not used to this kind of thing, after all.

"Slow down," I say softly to him.

He smiles down at me, then he moves between my legs, pulling my dress up to my waist. He kisses my thighs, his tongue moving up until it rests between my legs. His warm tongue moving rhythmically over and around my inner lips, his mouth sucking gently on my clit. The sensation is blowing my mind.

My hands are in his hair as I lean into it, my head falling against the pillow. Moans escape me in involuntary gasps. As his tongue moves inside me, fucking me gently, I feel myself getting close already.

But I don't want to come yet. Oh . . . wait . . . *not yet* .

. .

The feeling sweeps over me like a wave. My legs threaten to shut, but he grips my thighs, his strong arms holding me to him as he rides the wave of my vibrating body.

And to my surprise, when he lifts his head up, I'm far from sated. I want more.

I sit up and pull the dress off over my head as he undoes his shirt and takes off his pants. He barely gets it all off before I'm kissing his chest and straddling him. My mouth goes to his neck as his hands grasp my ass.

"I thought you wanted me to slow down," he says playfully.

I respond with a playful bite into his shoulder. He growls and pushes me down to the bed. I roll over with him, ending up on top again. I lean into him, my hands on his chest. He reaches up and cups my breasts, his thumbs running over my nipples, flicking them gently. He raises himself up, his tongue circling the nipple of my left breast, then sucking on it.

At the same time, he maneuvers me over his cock. As he enters me, he moans against my chest. Feeling him moving slowly inside me nearly sends me into orbit again. He grabs my hips and thrusts, animal growls escaping him with every pump of his hips.

"Oh, Xander," I say in a gaspy moan, "Oh yes . . . yes . . ."

Sharp claws dig into my hips, and the tingle of fangs prick my nipples. The little stings of pain combined with the pleasure is like heaven. My wolf is growing restless, and my own claws start to come out, digging into his chest.

He stops sucking my breast and moves his tongue up the center of my chest. "Don't hold back," he moans. "You can't hurt me."

I don't know about that, but I know that I'm close to coming. I look down and see my claws digging into him, and I pull back, putting my hands on either side of him. He notices right away and growls, fucking me harder.

"Don't hold back," he repeats through clenched fangs. "Give it to me, baby."

My wolf nearly comes out, but I hold it back. I lean into him, claws in his shoulders as I ride him, matching his speed and ferocity. Our moans of passion are becoming more like animal growls, and my legs are starting to shake violently.

I'm nearly coming, and I feel like I might lose all control. He grabs hold of me and flips me over. He lifts one of my legs and fucks me deep, his cock diving deep into me as I come a second time.

"You are mine," he growls into my ear. "My Thea . . . Oh yes . . . my Thea . . ."

He moans as he releases inside me. He slows down, kissing me gently. I wrap my legs around his waist. I hope this never ends.

I'm not sure how much time has passed . . . or even how many times I've come. I didn't know a person could come more than once in a night.

I'm lying here in Xander's arms, my head on his chest, listening to our synced heartbeats. Connection. This is what the elders were talking about.

"I almost lost control," I say softly to him.

"I know." He falls silent, then says, "You have nothing to worry about with me."

I chuckle. "Tell Rhiannon that."

He sighs. "You're not still thinking of what happened in training all those weeks ago, are you?"

I shrug. "I think if I sent you back to the infirmary, Olcan would never forgive me."

"There are worse ways to be injured." Another pause. Then, "I've wanted to do this again since our wedding night."

"Why didn't you?" I say as I raise my head to look at him.

He looks back with calmness in his eyes. The look of annoyance he would normally give me is long gone. It's now replaced with tenderness.

"I don't know." He slightly tilts his head in response. "Maybe I wasn't sure if it was what you wanted. Maybe I wasn't sure if this was what *I* wanted. This hasn't been a very easy path for us."

"No kidding." Sadness creeps into my heart as I realize what's to come. What we've been preparing for this whole time. "The Moon Comet is almost here," I say.

"Yes," he says, his voice so soft, it's almost a whisper.

"What if we're not ready? I mean, I don't know if I'm going to be ready in time to break the curse."

"Don't say that. You'll be ready."

I scoff. "I wish that I shared the faith you and the pack have in me. You all see me every day while I practice, and every day, I can see all of your hopes growing bigger. I mean, I'm picking all this up pretty fast, but will I be good enough? What if I'm not at the level I need to be to overcome this threat? It scares me to pieces."

He sits up and looks over at me, his brow furrowed. "Is that how you truly see yourself?"

I raise my eyebrows at his question. *Gee. How do I see myself?*

Like an outcast. Both in what could now be referred to as my former life and the thriller that is now my current life. I see myself as a girl who has just been going through life barely living in it, just existing and trying to make it through each day. A girl who barely made a dent in a world that was never for her and pulled into a world where it all depends on her.

I swallow, mulling over these thoughts.

"Like I am not suitable for all of this," I say, admitting to my low self-worth.

He brings a finger to my chin and tips my face up to him. "Thea," he says. "You are a wonder to everyone here. Never doubt the impact you can make. And as the Alpha and your mate, I will make sure that you are not alone in this. I will be with you every step of the way."

I think about what might happen if I do fail. The moon comet is supposed to fill all the wolves with great power. But the wolves that are cursed will use that power to ravage everyone. *Everyone.* This pack, this town, we'll all be destroyed.

He kisses me on my forehead, and I melt into him. For now, I'm here with him, and that is about as safe as we can ever be. In each other's arms.

Chapter Fourteen — Xander

It's time to discuss a solid game plan against the Shamans.

We're a month away from the Moon Comet's arrival, and while I don't know what role they will play on that day, I do know that if we all go mad, they will be there to hit us at our weakest point.

As I stand before my pack, I remember the battle we fought only a few days back. The way they seemed to appear out of nowhere, their magic further maddening us under the full moon. They did so much damage to the pack and to the people, and yet many of us still survived. I know the Shamans are much more powerful than that. I don't think they can overcome us just yet, but I know that more damage could have easily been done.

"If you ask me," Conan says when I bring up the battle, "we were more prepared than they expected us to be. We just put up a proper defense."

"I don't think so," I say. "From what we know of the Shamans, it seems unlikely that they would appear here to wipe us out before the arrival of the Moon Comet."

"Why else would they come here, then? There's no love lost between our people. Why wouldn't they try it now?"

There's a pause as everyone mulls the question over. Akila shakes her head slowly. "Xander's right," she says. "Strategically speaking, it doesn't make sense for them to come now."

"The Moon Comet," Branson says, his low voice rippling through air as he sits on the far end of our corner of the training field. "When it comes, we will have no control over ourselves. Our minds will be more easily manipulated by magic."

"Yeah, so?" says Conan. Branson's great brow deepens into a scowl.

"When you hunt, you seek out the biggest prey, right?"

"Of course. Big prey, better eating."

"Do you always hunt with that in mind?"

"Who doesn't? Of course, I do."

"Even if an easier opportunity presents itself? A young elk with his antlers stuck in tree branches, perhaps? You would run after its faster brethren instead of taking what has been handed to you?"

Conan looks impatient at this inquiry. "What's your point?"

"I think my point is clear."

Conan scowls at Branson, but I get his meaning. Before I can say anything, though, Thea speaks up.

"It was a scrimmage," she says. I look at her with confusion. "A test run. If the moon affects us in a similar way, they were probably looking to see how much resistance we would offer. Many of us survived, certainly, but a lot of us were injured, even killed . . . enough to give them some idea of what it'll be like when they come back in a month's time."

Of course. Thea's nailed it on the head. It was a test.

"So, how do we prepare?" Akila asks. "How *can* we prepare?"

I sigh and look around at the faces of the higher rank of my pack. It was a valid point. If we were weakened, we could only do so much against each other, much less the Shamans.

And then there's Thea. Our savior. She's almost ready. I see it in her training every day and the efforts she makes in being as perfect as perfect could get in time for the Moon Comet. She's been working hard physically and, as she just demonstrated, mentally. She's become sharp in her assessments.

But something is still holding her back. I can feel it as sure as I feel my own heartbeat. Fear? Uncertainty? I can't pinpoint it.

Thea has the drive. She has the voracity. She's taken her hits. That much is true. But she gets back up every time. Now, she's even bested Akila on more than one occasion. She's rapidly becoming an elite soldier in this pack. To hear her talk last night about her fears, though, I'd be lying if I said I didn't share them to some degree. I know enough of this life to know that sometimes, one can do everything right and still fail. And failure in this is just not an option. Our survival depends on our success.

"I think it's time Thea turned to the seers for a solution," I say.

Her eyebrows raise in surprise. "Me? Just me?"

I nod. "You are both wolf and Shaman. A connection with them could bring answers that even I would not find."

She looks at me with worried eyes, but nods valiantly just the same. "Of course."

"Well, what's all this? A welcome party for me? How charming." My attention shifts to Luther, who's walking toward us with a smile on his face and his arms spread.

"Nice of you to join us," I say bitterly. "We are in the middle of strategizing after the attack a few days ago."

His smile falters a little. "Yes, I heard. We lost a great many men and women. A tragedy."

Luther, of course, was absent at the time of the attack. He's barely ever around lately. Yes, he comes and goes as he pleases, but over the last week or so, he's been even more invisible than usual.

"Where were you the night of the attack?" I ask, and he shrugs.

"Elsewhere. I assure you, dear brother, I was safe from harm in the embrace of the many hard-working wenches at the maiden house at the edge of town." He says this with a casual laugh. Like this was any other day. Heat rises within me.

"Your place was here," I growl at him. "*Here*. Defending your pack."

The remainder of his smile disappears as he replies, "If I had known, I would have come, brother." We stare at each other for a long time before he finally tilts his head to one side. "You seem tense about all this. What do you say to a challenge? A friendly brawl to let off steam?"

Of course. He doesn't show his face for days, and now he's stopped everything because he wants to cause a spectacle. It looks like he's succeeded. Everyone's exchanging glances with one another, wondering if I'll bite. I am in no mood for this right now.

"I don't have time for games," I tell him. "There is work to be done."

"Yes, yes. There is always work to be done. I only suggest a break." He takes off his jacket. "Just a tussle among brothers. What do you say?"

He's standing there, eyebrows raised, a playful smile on his face.

Everyone has fixed their eyes on me to gauge my reaction. Despite his flippant attitude about things, I know that Luther always seems to have my best interest at heart . . . and maybe I do need to let off some steam. This entire thing has me wound tight.

I take off my jacket. "All right. One round."

I walk into the middle of the grounds. Everyone now has smiles on their faces, muttering and settling around us to watch. They so rarely get to witness the brothers battle. I wouldn't be surprised if they're also placing bets on who could drop whom first.

"Take it easy on me, brother," Luther says with a sly smile. "We all know you are the strongest here."

It starts light. We're throwing weightless punches, ducking and evading each other. Everyone watches with interest, some rooting for either of us with loud cheers sounding in the air.

But this feels simple. There are no complicated movements between us. Just playful rabbit punches and dodges. And I'm beginning to feel lighter, the way we used to when we play fought as cubs . . .

I throw a punch and he ducks, swinging around and wrapping me up in a rear bear hug. He's squeezing me a little too tight, but that's all right. I can get out of this easily. I grab his wrists and pull my weight down to break the hold. He releases me but then punches me hard in the ribs, sending me tumbling face forward into the dust. I land on my hands and knees, and there's a worried gasp from the pack around us.

I roll out of the way as his boot comes down hard in the dirt. He comes at me again, kicking at me and stomping at my arms and midsection, just barely missing me with each attack. I manage to get to my feet in time for him to crash into me, his elbow slamming into my side again. I take several steps back as the pain shoots through me and the air leaves my lungs. *What the hell?*

He takes another swing, but I dodge, catching his arm and twisting it around his back. I growl into his ear, "What the hell are you doing?"

"Fighting . . . you . . ." he pants. He then brings his elbow up to my face. I lean back to dodge, and that's enough for him to twist his arm out of my grip.

Friendly brawl, indeed. He dances around me, his smile turning sinister. "Come on, big brother," he jeers. "You're not tired yet, are you?"

I rush at him, and he slides to one side, kicking me hard in the shin. I tumble, falling forward onto one knee. "Say goodnight, brother." He gears up to kick me.

Suddenly, Luther goes flying off to one side. With lightning speed, Thea rushes onto the training grounds, tackling and pinning him to the ground. She grapples him with one arm around his neck while wrapping her legs around his thighs. He struggles, but she tightens her grip. He growls and gasps for air, but she's not letting him go.

"Thea!" I shout, but she's gone into that blank state she was in when she and Rhiannon fought all those weeks ago. Luther's lips are starting to turn blue as she squeezes, her fangs coming out as she clenches her teeth.

I rush over, grabbing her arms to pull her free. "Let him go! Thea!"

She snarls and tightens her hold. Luther's eyes start to glaze over. I reposition myself and grab her face, pulling her gaze to mine.

"Thea! Thea!" Her eyes are turning gold around the edges. I fear what will happen next if I don't free Luther now. I shake her. "Wake up!"

Her expression changes, the snarl dropping. The gold in her eyes starts to fade. "That's it. Come back to me, Thea. It's okay. I'm okay. You can let him go."

The gold fades away, and the fog around her eyes starts to clear. She blinks, focusing on me finally. Her grip loosens, and Luther leans forward, taking large gulps of air.

I help Thea to her feet as she looks back at Luther with wide, disoriented eyes. Luther, on the other hand, is still gasping and coughing, his hand at his throat. The pack has fallen silent around us, Thea's display once again bringing everyone into solemn reverence as Luther pulls himself together.

"Are you okay?" I ask him. He doesn't say anything as he gets to his feet. Conan, who happens to be close by, reaches out to assist. Luther slaps his hand away.

"Get your hands off me," he snaps. He straightens his dirt-covered shirt, then turns and staggers away without another word.

Around us, the pack rumbles with worry. Some watch after Luther, while others are looking to Thea and me. Rhiannon steps forward, her arms crossed tight around her chest. "Perhaps we should call it a day, Xander."

I nod and look at Thea. Her face is beet red as she avoids looking at anyone. She pulls away from me and starts walking toward the building. She's upset, as well she should be. This wasn't exactly how we planned this day to go.

I dismiss the rest of the pack, then follow her.

In our living room, Thea paces back and forth, muttering to herself. As soon as she sees me, she stops and shakes her head. "I suppose you're going to chastise me now for losing control again."

I don't have anything to say, really. I just see how upset she is right now.

"I knew there was something I didn't like about him," she says. "There is something rotten about him."

"Thea, Luther just got a little carried away. It happens sometimes—"

"No. Don't defend him. He was trying to hurt you."

"He wasn't. No more than you were trying to hurt Rhiannon."

I say that but instantly regret it. Her face turns red as she gapes at me in disbelief. "I can't believe you just said that."

"All I meant was that the heat of a battle can bring out the worst in a person. No one should know that better than you. Thank goodness I was there to prevent you—"

"Stop." She puts her hands up to me to stop me from talking. "Don't."

"Thea—"

"He could have hurt you, Xander. He was *trying* to hurt you. Don't you understand that? Luther does not have your best interests at heart."

I can understand how she feels this way. It must have been terrifying to see the battle get so out of control. But to jump to the conclusion that Luther means me harm . . .

"This was just training, Thea. I realize he should have backed off, but your response was not the best approach to the situation."

"Oh, it wasn't?" she says with a bitter laugh. "And what should I have done? Stand back and watch it happen? I don't think so."

It's like she's read my mind. I do wish she'd stayed out of it.

She shakes her head and adds, "I hate that I had to do what I did to him out there, but your life was in danger, Xander. How could you not see it? And he was grinning the whole time like he was playing kickball or something with your ribs."

"None of that matters, Thea. You simply can't keep doing this."

"This is just rich coming from you," she says haughtily. "If the situation were reversed—"

"It's not the same thing."

"It's exactly the same—"

"You could have killed him out there!" I explode.

She blinks at me. All the blood drains out of her face as she stares at me in shock.

"Thea," I reach out for her, but she pulls away, stepping back. Then, without a word, she turns and walks out of the room.

I exhale a sharp breath. Dammit. I shouldn't have said that. I'm not going to go after her. Not now. I'll talk to her when she's ready to listen.

Chapter Fifteen — Thea

I'm back in my old room this morning. After Xander made his position about his brother clear, I really didn't have *any* desire to see him anymore last night. You would think that his loyalties might lie a little closer to someone who actually cares about him.

I don't regret what I did. I don't know what Xander thought was happening, but he couldn't see Luther's face like I could. He was delighting in causing his brother pain.

I may have had doubts about him up until yesterday, but now I know that Luther is dangerous. Maybe Xander can't see it because he's his brother. I don't know. All I do know is that what I saw yesterday wasn't playful sibling banter. Luther displayed a kind of viciousness that set everything within me on alert. What happened after . . . Well, I could barely control what happened after.

I get up from my bed and go about getting washed and dressed. My mind replays everything that happened yesterday. This situation stinks. It stinks to high—

Everything falls away as I stand in my bathroom. The walls around me darken and disappear. When the light returns, I'm standing in a bloody battlefield with dead bodies littered all around me. Rivers of blood all around, mixing with the dirt and running off in tiny rivulets down the raised and hilly land. I start to walk through it all, the dead faces of the people of our clan as they lie on the ground staring up into the sky, to somewhere beyond this plane.

This is the work of the Shamans. I don't see any of them here, but I know that this is their doing. I see the decapitated heads of my clan, lying next to their naked forms. They had been wolves when they were killed.

I think of Xander. I can still feel him somewhere beyond the hovering smoke hanging over the field. He's alive. But where is he? Is he hurt? Captured?

I call out for him, and with every moment that passes, my hands shake with panic. What if my senses are lying to me, and he's dead? I am his Luna. I should know. But where *is he?*

"Thea!"

I turn to see Xander walking through the smoke. It seems like he's moving in slow motion toward me. My heart jumps, and I run toward him as fast as my legs can carry me.

We are only a few steps from each other when he abruptly stops. His eyes widen and his mouth becomes slack as he stiffens in front of me.

"Xander?" Before I can register what's happening, he falls to his knees. I rush to him, grabbing him as he slumps forward against me. I'm holding him up as best as I can, but I can feel the life draining out of him. "No. No, no, no."

He falls over onto my lap, his eyes looking out into nothingness. His body is warm in my arms, but he's gone. *Oh, no, please! Please don't be dead . . . please . . .*

I don't have time to cry. A pair of feet steps forward into my eyeline. A large, bloody sword hangs by the figure's legs. As my eyes travel upward, I see a man standing over me, a black cloak covering his face. I open my mouth to scream, and everything goes dark again.

I wake up on the floor of my bathroom.

With tears in my eyes, my legs and hands shaking, I slowly get to my feet. I need to find someone. Xander, Gemma, somebody . . .

I go to the bedroom and start getting dressed, my shaky hands struggling with the buttons of my pants. I try taking deep breaths. I can't go raving through the halls like a lunatic.

I leave my room, still trying to control my breathing. Gemma should be with the seers right about now. She speaks with them nearly every morning. They'll know what to do.

I find them in the large meeting room. Gemma and the seers stand around a large table. As I walk in, they all turn to look at me. A half-second passes before Gemma steps forward, reading the obvious panic in my eyes.

"Thea?" she says, "What is it? Are you okay?"

"A vision," I reply in a small, shaky voice. "I just saw a vision."

"Oh, my dear." Gemma pulls me into her arms and leads me to the ring of couches on the side of the room. "Come, come. Come sit."

I sit down and try to collect myself. I hate this.

The seers move toward me in unison, their long cloaks making them look as if they're floating. Gemma sits next to me and takes my hand.

"Tell us what you saw, dear."

I tell it all. The battlefield, the bloodied bodies . . . and Xander dying in my arms. Every eye is on me, silently listening until I'm done. And the silence continues for a long moment after. The seers exchange worried glances, and Gemma isn't looking at me.

"What does it mean?" I ask.

Gemma pauses, then turns her eyes down to my hands. One of the seers speaks up.

"Your vision is troubling, but if we were to guess, what you saw was a future that could come to pass once the Moon Comet arrives."

My mouth goes dry. I hadn't wanted to think that's what I saw—the aftermath of the Moon Comet's effect on the clan. I take a deep, shaky breath. I would do anything to go back to being a normal person. The "seer" part of my whole Daywolf thing is enough to make me want to throw up.

"It was like my nightmares," I say. "Except...except this time I was awake. It was so real."

"Your visions are more intense now," says another seer. "It is nothing to be afraid of. You are offering us a well-needed warning."

I just shake my head. "A warning?" I reply. "A warning that we're all going to die?"

"These shadows do not have to stand as you saw them," Gemma says. "There is still time to change the outcome."

I release a deep breath, and chills rush up my spine. "So what do we do now? What next?"

"We need to speak with my son," Gemma explains, "and discuss this vision. There might be clues within it that may lead us to a solution."

I take in her words and, with it, just a bit of hope for our future. With her gentle smile, she adds, "We will get through this together. You are not alone, Thea. This clan is your family now, and family protects each other."

My eyes sting with tears. After everything in the last twenty-four hours, it feels good to hear someone say that. Even if it wasn't Xander.

After all that's happened, I go back to bed. I've been sleeping for who knows how long, and now as I rise back up into consciousness, I realize that Xander is standing outside my door. Who knows how long he's been there? I sigh and sit up in my bed. I wish he would just come in if he wants to talk to me.

"Stop standing outside like a stalker and get in here," I shout. It's a few seconds before the door slowly opens. Xander stands on the threshold of my room, looking at me with careful eyes and holding his arms behind his back. He's hanging his head slightly, and it occurs to me that he looks more like a large dog that's been chastised than his usual Alpha role.

He steps over the threshold finally and walks to the center of the room, giving me my space. "I just left an urgent meeting with the seers," he says. "They told me about your vision."

I just stare at him, waiting for whatever it is that he really wants from me. He adds, "Are you all right?"

The image of him falling into my arms appears in the forefront of my mind. I push it away. "I'm better now."

He nods, his silver-ringed eyes shaking a little as he regards me. "I am so sorry I was not here with you."

The way he looks at me now . . . his eyes are glassy, but he's not crying. Instead, worry takes over his countenance, and my heart twists at the thought of him agonizing over my well-being.

"These visions—" I begin, then stop. I don't really know how to express how terrible it really was. He waits for me to gather my thoughts in silence.

"I'm so frightened, Xander," I say to him finally. "It was so real. I . . . I . . ."

He walks over to me and sits on the bed, brushing my hair out of my eyes. "They're just visions. Little more than nightmares."

"Sure," I say with a scoff. "Except they could come true."

"But they don't have to. They can remain in the realm of dreams. All we need to do is make sure they never come to pass."

"You sound so sure of yourself. How can you be so certain?"

One corner of his mouth turns up in a smile, and he says, "I have faith in you and what you can do. I know a way will be made for us because our lives cannot end here. Not when there's still so much for us to become."

My heart fills with warm light as he speaks. Still, he believes in me, even as I do my best to grasp all the new powers I possess. I can hardly believe his unwavering faith.

I lean into him and kiss him, his soft lips pressing against mine. Our kiss evolves as our tongues meet and dance together. I run my hands through his hair as he leans into me, laying me down on the bed.

I no longer remember why I was mad at him. I barely remember the fear in my heart from only a few hours ago. As he undoes my nightgown and his tongue moves over my hardening nipples, I forget it all. He's all I've ever wanted . . . all I've ever needed.

"Thea . . . my Thea," he whispers as he moves on top of me and kisses my neck. I undo his shirt, my hands delighting in the muscles of his chest. His shirt comes off, then pants. My nightgown rides up, and his hips are between my legs.

The bliss of how he fills me up takes me. His hips move slowly as he moans against my mouth.

And I think, maybe for the first time, *I love this man.*

I wrap my legs around his waist as he fucks me slow and hard just the way I like it. When my body finally gives into him, I melt in his arms.

I am his, and he is mine. Forever and ever. Let no one tear us asunder.

Chapter Sixteen — Xander

"The dark figure should be our focus, Alpha."

We're a few days out from the Moon Comet, and Thea and I have been waiting for a response from the seers about her vision. In the meantime, we've been preparing for the worst as best we can. The safe house has been stocked, and every wolf who cannot fight has been assigned to be taken there on the day of the comet. I don't know how much good it will do once the comet's here. Still, I have to try to protect everyone.

Now, the seers stand before me. We're in my living room, and Thea is sitting on the edge of the chair next to me. Her brow furrows slightly. "The dark figure from my dream?"

The seers all nod in unison. "The curse hangs over us because of the division between the Shaman and wolf clans. Therefore, the Eldest Shaman must make a blood offering to our clan on the night of the Moon Comet to break the curse."

Thea and I exchanged glances. I ask, "That's what you got out of her vision? How are we supposed to find the Eldest Shaman with only a few days left?" I can't help but notice how nervous they all look. They're all shifting around like children in trouble. "What?"

"That is but one possible interpretation," the one elder says. "You being struck down . . . It suggests a failure that you do not see coming. Something that you have not prepared for."

I can feel Thea's worried glare on me. I clench my jaw, chasing away my own fear. "What steps must we take to locate this Shaman?"

"Xander," Thea began, but I put my hand up to silence her.

"I can only worry about what I know, Thea," I say to her. "Not what may happen. Not at this stage." I look back to the seers, and another of them clears their throat.

"We know they gather outside of our borders. It seems they are preparing as well. When the Shaman is found, he will need to be weakened. That is where you come in, Luna. As it has been foretold, it must be you to end the curse."

I see Thea blink. She's still not used to her title of Luna, so it takes her a second, but she finally nods.

"Fine," I say. "Have my generals join us in the meeting room."

The seers leave after that. I get up from my place on the couch, grabbing my jacket to leave.

"Hey," Thea says, her voice a little shaky with fear. "Is this really the best plan of action? I mean, what if—"

"It is," I say it firmly. "It has to be. Are you ready?"

"No, but I don't have any other choice, do I?"

I walk over to her and pull her into my arms, kissing her on the forehead. "We can do this. I promise you."

She looks up at me and smiles. I know she believes it because I believe it. We have to succeed. It's the only path.

On the way to the meeting room, I pass through the halls and immediately notice the nervous unrest among my pack. Everyone is either walking on eggshells around each other or panicking about what that day might mean for us. Not that I could blame any of them. Whatever we do now will ultimately decide our future.

When we get to the meeting room, Rhiannon, Conan, Akila, and Branson are all standing in wait for us already. Rhiannon's eyes flicker to Thea by my side. She stiffens a little but makes no comment about her presence. In the months since everything happened, Rhiannon has been focusing on her duties more and more. It's made her a better soldier, but I can't help but wonder about how things will fall once the chaos starts.

As I sit down with everyone, I explain what the seers found. Everyone at the table listens in silence, the gravity of the situation now clear among us all. When I'm finally done, Rhiannon speaks first.

"So we have to bring the battle to them? Sounds like a foolish plan given that most of us will have trouble keeping ourselves under control."

"We have to try, though," says Akila. "If it's our only hope. Does anyone have a better idea?" No one spoke up. "Well, then, let's form a plan of attack. Once the eldest has been located, I say we converge upon that area with a sneak attack."

I nod in agreement. "Rhiannon, I want you to be on point with this."

"All right. If I may make a suggestion," Rhiannon pauses, glancing over at Thea, "I can take a small force in as a distraction. Then you and Thea can capture the Eldest Shaman."

"Capture?" Thea nearly laughs. "I don't know about that. He's supposed to be the most powerful of them, right? That sounds like suicide."

"I will protect you," I tell her. "You won't have to worry about that."

"Well, sure, but what about you? If you can take this guy all alone, then what are we even doing right now? Someone should have your back, too."

I think about that for a moment. Thea's not wrong. I'm a powerful wolf, but just me standing between the Eldest Shaman and certain destruction does sound like a suicide mission.

"Fine," I say. "Luther will come with us."

Thea's face blanches, but she looks away. She's still distrustful of Luther, clearly. I wait for her objection, but she only says, "All right. If you're sure about it . . . then okay."

So that's the plan. Rhiannon and our forces will cause a distraction in their camp, and Luther, Thea, and I will get the Shaman's blood to end the curse. I look at Thea and I can see her worry, but I'm not going to let anyone touch her. That is my duty as her mate and the Alpha. I'm going to protect her with every fiber of my being.

"All right," I tell everyone. "Make yourselves ready." We all stand. As everyone else is leaving, Rhiannon steps up to me.

"May I speak to you in private, my Lord?"

I can feel Thea's eyes on me, and I start to tell her no. Thea's hand on my arm stops me. "I'm going to go meditate. See you later."

I look down at Thea, who smiles warmly at me in understanding. There's a fence that needs to be mended here.

The room empties and Rhiannon says, "I never thought that this is where we would end up. I always thought I'd be the one fighting by your side."

"That hasn't changed. You are still my best warrior."

She doesn't smile at this. She only stares, her eyebrows tipped up in sadness. "I've had a lot of time to think about everything, and I don't know if I'll ever be completely all right with you and Thea . . . but I must respect it." She looks away, glancing down at the table for a moment before returning her eyes back to me, "You know, the world where Thea comes from, they don't put a lot of stock in destiny. They prefer to try to control every element of their lives. When she first arrived, I was a little jealous that I didn't come from a place like that. I thought that maybe if I could seize some control over things, then I wouldn't have to lose you."

She pauses, and I don't fill the silence. I give her the space to speak her mind.

"Then somewhere along the way, I realized that I haven't lost you. You're still here, and so am I. Our paths were chosen long before we were even born. Who am I to deny the Moon Goddess's wisdom? Especially when I see how happy you are with her."

Her blue eyes start to rim with water. With a crooked smile, she steps close to me and kisses me on the cheek.

"I love you, Xander," she says softly. "And when you love someone, you want all the happiness in the world for them. I know now that you have that with Thea. It would be wrong of me to deny you that. When this is all done, I will stand at the side of my Alpha and my Luna, as is my destiny."

Her smile widens a little as tears run down her cheeks. Then she steps back and walks out of the room without another word.

Thea sits on the side of the compound with her eyes closed and her back rod straight. She's as still as a statue, her heartbeat as slow as if she were sleeping. I almost turn away, but she opens her eyes and smiles at me the second I do.

"Hey," she says. She pats the ground next to her. "Sit with me."

I do and I lean in and kiss her, joyful to have another moment in her presence. Her devotion to all of this is commendable and very attractive. She no longer acts like an outcast. She seems to fit right in with everyone else now.

"So," she asks, "how is the plan going?"

"Just received word from our scouts about a possible location of the Eldest Shaman. Rhiannon's gathering the troops."

She nods and looks away from me, then takes a deep breath. "I guess this is really happening, then. You know, all this talk about me weakening the Shaman . . . I don't know how I'm going to do that. I know the seers said I would know when the time comes, but this whole 'blind faith' thing is new to me."

"I know," I say, taking her hand in mine. "But you are powerful, and this is your destiny. We have to believe that we can't fail."

She nods and leans her head on my shoulder. "You really are my safe place."

Her words almost crush my heart. My feelings for Thea are completely different from where we started. I think about Rhiannon's words about destiny and the Moon Goddess knowing best and . . . and I guess there is truth in that. I cannot imagine a life without Thea now.

"I am honored," I say with a smile.

"Thank you for everything you've done for me. You saw in me what I couldn't see in myself, and that helped me to keep going. I'm nervous about all this, but I feel like I have a chance."

"No need to thank me." I kiss her on the forehead. "Come on. Let's find Luther and get going with this plan."

She stands up with me, and we head back to where Rhiannon was gathering the soldiers. It occurs to me then that I might not have another chance, so I stop, pulling Thea back to me and embracing her.

"If we were ever to meet in another life, I would wish that it did not have to take a war to bring us together." My eyes moved between hers. "I cannot promise that we will all come out of this alive, but I can promise that I will protect you with everything I've got, even if it costs me my last breath. I want you to know that I . . . I love you, Thea. And no matter what happens tomorrow, I will always love you."

Tears hang in her eyes as she presses her lips against mine.

"I love you too, Xander," she whispers against my lips. "And I'm glad that you'll be there to protect me. I didn't come all this way just to lose you at the end, so I'll be there to protect you, too. I can't do this without you."

I glow with pride at her bravery. My mate, my Luna, my everything.

Chapter Seventeen — Thea

The night of the Moon Comet, everything's in place. I've never been more terrified.

The plan seems simple on paper. Rhiannon will lead her forces in while Xander, Luther, and I sneak in through the back of their camp to the Eldest Shaman's hut. As night falls, we leave as wolves, a small army of us set to launch a precise strike. With every step that we take toward the border, my heart pounds like a drum.

When we reached the edge of their camp, Rhiannon, Xander, Luther, and I all changed to humans and hunkered down on the ridge just above it. Now, I'm looking out at all the huts. Just about every one is dark as the sky moves into night.

"The Moon Comet will appear just over the horizon a few minutes after the sun sets," says Rhiannon. "You'll have until the moon's peak to get the Eldest Shaman's blood and perform the ritual. That won't take long. The comet moves fast."

I can't take my eyes off the dark huts. Shouldn't they be awake? It's not that late yet.

"Brother," Luther says to Xander, "let me take point. I should be the one to lead us in once we reach the Shaman."

My stomach tightens. I don't like the idea of Luther doing anything. I guess Xander doesn't either because he replies, "You'll back us up. Keep watch. Make sure no one sneaks up on us."

Luther agrees, and I realize that the plan sounds even worse than the one that Luther just suggested. Still, I'm no military strategist. I'll have to keep my eye on Xander myself.

"Let's go," says Rhiannon. She looks at us both and nods her head sharply. "Good luck."

She shifts and returns to the rest of the pack. As they move off, the three of us shift and start moving in the direction of the Eldest Shaman's hut with soft but quick steps.

We weave around the huts quietly, making sure that we don't make a sound. As wolves, we can see better in the dark and keep to the path that we'd mapped out. It doesn't take us long to find the Eldest Shaman's hut. Flanked outside his door are two wolves from the Gorg Clan. Large and intimidating, they sit by the entrance like giant guard dogs.

Xander moves forward, but I hesitate. Something isn't right about this, but I can't put my finger on it. Luther comes up behind me and mind-links, *What is it?*

There shouldn't be guards. I almost say that to him, but I hold back. Maybe this is normal for someone as important as the Eldest Shaman.

Nothing, I reply. I hear Xander mind-link to Luther.

You take the one on the left. I'll take the one on the right.

Obediently, Luther follows Xander. The two sneak around the wolves, then leap on them in unison, tearing out their throats in a coordinated attack. Xander turns his massive head to me in the darkness and mind-links, *Come on, let's go.*

We push the door open, and again that nervous feeling nags at me. An unlocked door, wolves guarding the entrance, dark huts as far as the eye can see . . .

We walk into the first room to find bedding and bags, belongings of the Eldest Shaman, but no one is here.

Confused, the three of us stand there, looking around and sniffing for any clue of the Shaman.

This doesn't make sense. The scouts assured us he'd be here. Could they have been mistaken?

Luther, Xander mind-links, *stay by the door*.

Luther rushes off and through the door to stand guard. I change back to human, and Xander follows suit. "I don't understand it. Why isn't he here? What do we do?"

My heart is pounding, and my breath is getting shallow. I'm excited, but suddenly I feel a little too excited. Xander is starting to pant a little as well. It's the Moon Comet. Rhiannon said that it wouldn't take long to reach its peak.

"We're running out of time," he says. "We need to find him."

Before we can say anything, we hear fighting somewhere near us. The distraction. Shit. Xander says, "Let's search the nearby huts. He can't have gotten far."

We both change to wolves, and Xander mind-links to Luther as we walk out, *We're going to look for—*

We get outside and Luther's gone. We both look around for a second, then scent the air. He's not far, but what the hell?

Xander, this isn't good, I mind-link to him.

I know. Come on.

We rush to the sound of fighting. Shamans are shooting their magic at the army of wolves in the center of their camp. The battle is on, and it looks like we're winning. The Shamans in their long white robes, staffs in hand to defend themselves are all backing away. Xander starts to leap into battle, but I stop him. I can't hold back any longer.

Xander, look at them. Why are there so few?

He blinks at me, his gold-glowing eyes narrowing. *What?*

The Shaman! There should be more of them. Why aren't there?

He turns and looks at the wolf pack fighting the Shaman, and he takes a step back. He sees it. Something isn't right here.

Just as he makes that realization, several of the wolves wince in pain, twisting and writhing and howling as if something had just grabbed hold of them. I look up to see the silvery glow of the Moon Comet above us, almost at the center of the sky.

I can feel its power. Rage starts to build inside me. All I want is to tear something apart. To hurt someone . . . something . . .

Xander jumps into my eyeline. *Stay with me,* he mind-links.

He changes to human, and that makes me change too. He takes me by the shoulders and says, "Resist it. We're almost through this."

"It's a trap," I say breathlessly. "Don't you see? They lured us here so that we'll run out of time."

I can see the questions in Xander's eyes, but there's no time. He's suddenly knocked over by a large wolf.

Chaos ensues as our pack starts to attack one another, giving way to the power of the comet above us. I look on in horror as the remaining Shamans run for the caves, and my pack dissolves before me. For a few seconds, I don't know what to do or how to move. The comet's power thrums through me, and for just a second, I want to join the fray.

Then I close my eyes and take a deep breath. I can't let this happen. I can't let my pack die this way.

I scream. The sound cuts through the air, grabbing hold over every wolf before me. The battle comes to a halt. Wolf snarls drop and expressions flatten.

I stand there looking at all of them with tears in my eyes. Xander is the first to get up and rush over to me. "Are you—"

"I'm fine," I say, wiping at my face. I don't feel like it's over. The rumbling of anger still swirls inside me. "We need to get everyone to safety."

"Not before we put an end to this once and for all." Xander turns to the others. "Rhiannon, Conan, get everyone to the safe house. Now. Akila, Branson, on me."

We rush to the caves, changing to wolves as we do. It's harder to resist the pull of the Moon Comet like this, but we need to move fast. We get to the cave's entrance, and I hear voices and movement deep within the darkness beyond.

They're inside, Xander mind-links. We rush inside and immediately see the remaining Shamans running down a path with at least four Gorg pack wolves. We're in hot pursuit.

The path opens up into a cavern, where the Eldest Shaman slowly stands as we approach. The Shamans and the wolves all surround him, ready for anything.

We stand at the exit, growls filling the air, and all I can think is that we don't have time for this.

I can hear their heartbeats. All of them. I focus on that, drawing the power from the Moon Comet within me to help me control it. Seconds pass and I see them all start to crumble, grabbing their chests and falling to their knees.

Xander and the others change to human and watch in disbelief as all of them fall into a slump.

"Good Goddess," Akila whispered.

I pull back as I hear their heartbeats slow to a crawl, and I change back to human. Xander doesn't waste any time. He walks over to the Eldest Shaman.

"The Moon Comet is almost at its peak. I can feel it," Akila says. "We're out of time."

Xander sighs and pulls out a dagger from the belt of the Eldest Shaman. "We'll have to do it here, then," he says.

Branson finds a water flask on one of the other Shamans and kneels down next to Xander as he lifts the Eldest's arm up to slice his wrist open. It wasn't a chalice, and this wasn't a ritual space, but it was going to have to do for the moment. I stay back, watching them, ready for if any of them try to wake up.

Xander slices into the Shaman's veins, and as soon as the blood starts to run into the flask, I feel someone behind me.

A hand comes up and wraps itself around my neck. I freeze as my attacker yanks me back and grabs my arms with his free hand, binding them behind me.

"You just had to save the day, didn't you, Thea?" A voice growls in my ear.

Xander, Akila, and Branson's attention turns sharply to me. They all freeze for a moment, then Xander releases the Eldest Shaman's hand and stands slowly.

"Luther."

"Hello, big brother."

All time has stopped around us. Luther's claws dig into my skin. "What have you done?" Xander growls.

"What I was born to do," he replies.

I'm looking at Xander, watching for any sign of attack or defense. Akila and Branson shoot glances at one other, telegraphing silent orders.

"You have led this path to their destruction for the final time," he goes on. "You had your chance as Alpha, now I shall take mine as the new Alpha King."

Xander narrows his eyes at him. "What are you talking about? You betrayed me for power? Is that it?"

"Once the rest of our pack gives in to the Moon Comet's power, the Shamans will lead us to victory in an assault on Clarion. Tonight is only the beginning of our reign."

The fury in Xander's eyes is palpable, but I can also feel his hurt. He truly believed Luther would never betray him this way.

"We have been resolved to rule over this tiny town when we have the blood of kings!" Luther shouts. "You may be satisfied as Alpha, but I will never be. It ends tonight."

Xander looks at me, and his eyes soften. He looks back at Luther. "Release her . . . and I will join your crusade."

Akila and Branson both look up at him, still crouched and waiting, but I imagine they're hoping he's joking. Luther laughs.

"I would be a fool to let her live," he says, "and a bigger fool to believe you."

Akila and Branson both stand in unison. Luther's claws press into my neck.

I wince with pain, and Xander puts a hand up behind him. "Stay back," he says.

"Control your dogs, or else your beloved Luna will lose her head." Luther's growls, a deep, deadly tone assaulting my ears.

"You don't have to do this. Just let her go. Let this be between us." Xander then turns his eyes to me and adds, "You don't have the *heart* to do this."

My eyes widen, and an understanding comes over me. I put all the others to sleep. Why couldn't I do that with Luther?

"Don't test me, Xander," Luther says, and suddenly, I'm aware of his heartbeat against my back. "I will kill her."

"You betrayed your family, your pack," Xander goes on. "You betrayed *me*, when I have done nothing but love you as my brother."

"You never loved me! You were always so concerned with everything else in this pack. You never even noticed me! You—"

He stops, and his grip loosens slightly. I have his heart in my control. I squeeze it in my invisible grip. It beats hard and fast, trying to survive.

"No," he gasps. His hands tighten momentarily, but it's no use. I'm not going to let it go. He starts gasping for breath, and suddenly, I'm freed from his grip. I stumble forward, whirling around on him, still holding his heart.

He falls to his knees, reaching out to me as he gasps. "Don't . . . do this . . ." he rasps, his dark hair in his eyes. Suddenly, I remember my nightmare. The man with the dark hair. The one I mistook for Xander. It was never him. Never him at all.

"You were supposed to be my salvation," he snarls. "Not theirs. They promised...they *promised*."

I have no sympathy for him. He almost killed us all. I have to make sure he never does it again.

"It's like you said before," I say to him, "We always have a choice, and you've left me with the only one I could choose. You will not hurt this pack again."

I push out all the power that's left in me, and his heart explodes in his chest. He roars out in pain, his hands turning to claws as he falls over onto the ground face first.

We stand there for a long few seconds before I feel Xander's hand on my shoulder. He hands me the flask of blood and says, "The time is nigh."

I nod. I take the flask and close my eyes, pouring the power within me through the leather and into the Shaman's blood. In my mind, I see a vision of a wolf man and a Shaman woman, walking with their child hand in hand.

Xander takes my hand and uses the dagger to make a cut in my palm. As the power of the comet reaches its zenith, he pours the blood over my hand. The power pulses through me, and my mind swirls within the memories of a million Shamans . . .

And I see her. Tall and bright in the sunlight. She smiles at me and nods. *Bring them together.*

The world feels like it's shaking all around me. There's a flash of light, then the energy flies out of me and into the sky.

When the light dies away, I'm on my knees with Xander before me. The rage inside me is gone. Xander touches my face gently.

"It worked!" I hear Akila say. "I don't feel like ripping anybody's head off!"

I smile, and Xander kisses my forehead. "Let's go home."

Epilogue — Thea

The celebration must have been going on for days. The music and dancing and food and drinks just flow endlessly. My mind has been spinning the whole time. It's as though the world is celebrating with us.

It's the last big dinner, as decreed by Xander and everyone here. Our entire pack (and even those from other packs!) have come to partake in the celebration. I was half expecting to see Xander's royal cousin, the Alpha King, and his Luna to show up, but no such luck. They did send gifts and many messages from Clarion's central city, however.

I'm thinking of all that lies ahead. On the subject of the Alpha King, Xander is planning on meeting with him soon to assist in a big undertaking—garnering peace between the Shaman nations and ours. He's the first Alpha in his line for generations who'll have to have these talks on a serious level. I'll be at his side. My presence is probably the most important part of all that. I think I should be feeling important, but really, I feel a little foolish about it all. Like a fangirl about to meet a king.

But then, I'm royalty now as well. Wow, this has been such a ride.

Right now, I'm sitting next to Xander, who's been pleasant but quiet for most of the evening. I can't blame him. This is a good day, but it's a hard one. He lost his brother, after all. I reach over and squeeze his hand gently. He smiles at me.

"It was for the best," he says, as if reading my mind.

"He was still your brother."

He nods. "Yes. For what it's worth, he was still that."

I look over at Xander, and I realize that he needs something to bring him back from his grief, even if it's just for tonight. This is a grand day, and if the Alpha isn't smiling, then, well . . .

Gosh, I'd been planning on telling him in private. It feels like I've been holding onto this information for ages. I suppose a celebration is a celebration, after all, and there will never be a better time than now to let the world know.

I stand up, and the entire room immediately falls silent. Right. I'm the Luna. My word is powerful. I clear my throat.

"I just wanted to say that today is a day that will be remembered for generations to come. Our names will be written down as the people who fought to keep their bloodline alive and who worked to join what never should have been torn apart. Every single one of us here today did their part, and that is why we are able to celebrate this night."

There was a loud uproar, followed by shouts of "Here, here!"

"We should not forget those who have lost their lives in our quest for survival. Their names will never be forgotten. We should also celebrate the beginning of a new life for this pack and for this town. No longer cursed, we can flourish the way we have always meant to." I look over at Xander and I touch my belly. "And I shall lead the charge in welcoming the first generation of the Crescent Pack to be born free from the curse."

It takes him and everyone else a few seconds to realize what I mean. Finally, his eyes drift to my belly, and his face splits into a warm smile.

"You are . . . with child?"

I nod. He has a look on his face like he's about to explode. He stands up like a shot, joyfully raising his mug while wrapping one arm around my waist, pulling me close. "May we flourish the way we were meant to!"

Everyone cheers. Xander looks down at me, love in his eyes. He pulls me into a kiss and everything around us falls away. In this moment, we are the only ones in the room.

It's not until I hear Rhiannon speak up above the cheers that our lips part. "To the Alpha and his Luna!"

She's smiling at us both, the approval of what was meant to be accepted in her eyes. We are truly a pack now. Truly a family. Our love, this land, this family. It's all I've ever wanted.

"Goddess, I love you so much, Thea." Xander leans his head into me, and I take his face in my hands.

"I love you, Xander."

To think, this story began with me wanting nothing more than to get out of that sorry little Podunk town and maybe find some adventure. Funny how I found all that I ever dreamed in the strangest of places. Xander and I kiss under the howls of joy from our subjects. I am greater than I ever thought I could be. This journey, for better and for worse, has brought me all that I could ever need or want.

To my Alpha, from his Luna, may we live always under the Moon Goddess' grace.

Did you like this book? Then you'll LOVE ***Alpha's One-Night Stand***:

I have a one-night stand with a gorgeous playboy on my first night at Moonhelm Academy. He says I'm his fated mate but I don't belong to anyone, especially not a wolf shifter.

Turn the page for a special preview.

Special Preview — Alpha's One-Night Stand

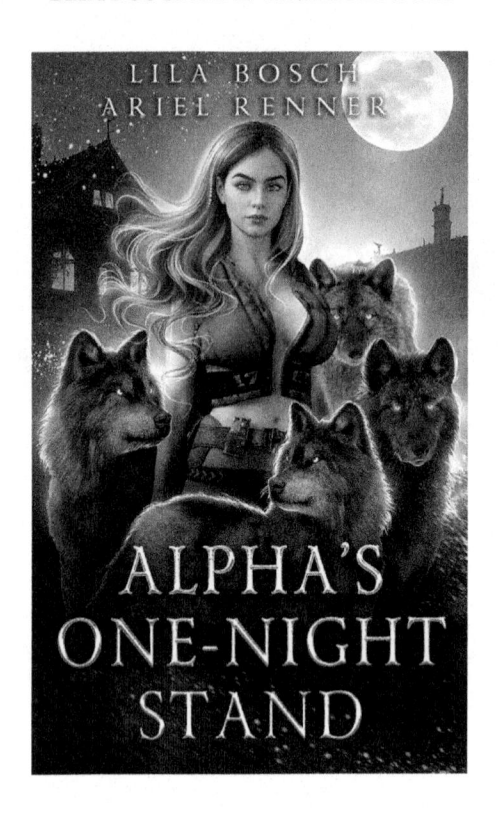

Chadwick

"Stand down," I say out loud once I'm alone. "Stand the fuck *down*." My wolf creeps into my voice now, an ancient growl mixing with my human tones. A sure signal that my wolf can burst out at any moment. I shut my eyes tight and start taking deep breaths. It starts to work. The wolf is backing down.

Fuck. This woman and her damnable scent are going to drive me insane.

I can't take it anymore. Somewhere in the night, her scent got stronger, permeating the walls of my room as if they were awash with it. I feel like I'm drowning in it. I can't take it anymore. I have to leave. I have to find her.

Nothing in this world ever gets me running unless I'm fighting or defending my territory. Yet, here I am, my heart pounding in my chest, my shoes crushing the damp grass, bounding across campus, and damn well praying that I don't lose the scent. My nose to the air, I'm closing in on it. I can feel it.

The sun is slowly hovering over the horizon, and the air around me is filled with the excitement of the Awakening Fest. I barely notice it. All that matters is that I find her.

I'm being led toward the campus bar. Moonlight, it's called. I get to the door and look up at the blinking sign. I don't sense too many other heartbeats beyond the door. I imagine everyone's getting ready for the ceremony. I enter the bar, and my suspicions prove correct. The bar is almost empty, save a few people, scattered around.

I scan the room, my senses heightened. It doesn't take long before I see a flash of electric purple out of the corner of my eye.

She's sitting on a bar stool, her back to me. Her waves of shiny purple hair pull me in along with that sweet smell. I've found her. Finally.

I walk toward her, and I can hear her heart beating. It's speeding up, syncing with mine. I clench my fists, pushing the wolf back down inside me. I'm a few steps away when she turns suddenly, making me take a step back. Her crystal blue eyes meet mine, and all the air leaves the room. A bit of her amethyst locks move effortlessly around her face, framing it as she puckers her lips slightly.

We stare at each other for a long moment before she slurs, "Who are you?" Her voice buzzes in my chest, striking the wolf within.

"I'm Chadwick," I reply, trying to keep my tone steady despite the surge of emotion pulsing through me.

She raises an eyebrow. "Chadwick," she repeats slowly, as if testing the name on her tongue. "Are you following me, *Chad*?"

I blink. "Following you?"

"The airport. You sat next to me, remember?"

I smile and take a seat next to her. "How could I forget? Your scent enraptured me the moment I picked it up."

She frowns and cocks her head like she doesn't understand. Then she laughs. "You Moonhelm dudes are weird AF."

She's messing with me. Interesting. I've had at least two women throw themselves at me since I started this trip, and this woman, with a scent that is driving the wolf inside me wild, appears to be unaffected by my presence. How very odd.

"I had to find you. I was drawn to you. I believe that you are meant to be mine."

She snorts and starts laughing loudly. "Is that supposed to be some kind of pickup line? Come on, man. You can do better than that."

She turns to me and takes my hand, leaning into me and looking me in my eyes as her fingers caress the palm of my hand. "You are the most beautiful woman I've ever seen," she says in a low, sultry voice. "When I walked in, I just had to say hello to you. You are a vision." She tosses my hand back to me. "*That's* how you pick up a girl. Try again, sport."

I'm shocked silent. I've never been thrown off so easily before. "What's your name?" I ask her.

"Yarra." She looks back at me and studies me for a long moment, as if weighing some imaginary options. "Buy me a drink?"

I raise an eyebrow and smile at her. "Sounds like you've already had a few too many."

She looks back at her half-empty glass and shrugs. "Eh, maybe. It's been a weird day."

"You don't say."

She nods, finishes the drink in one swallow, then orders another. "You wouldn't believe what I've been through. I'm actually not surprised that you're here hitting on me." She gets her drink and takes a sip, then turns to me and asks, "What cologne are you wearing?"

"What?"

"Your cologne? It smells really good, by the way. I don't think I've ever smelled anything like it."

She surprises me, but I'm smiling. There's something endearing about how easily she speaks to me. As if she doesn't realize our connection.

"Yarra," I say, "I think we should get to know each other." My wolf is starting to pace again. It's making me antsy, and my foot starts to tap to some unknown beat. "Or at least go somewhere more private."

She nods sagely. "That's a little better. Much better than the whole 'You're meant to be mine' thing."

"You are meant to be mine." I don't think there's any denying that now that I'm next to her. My mind is starting to whirl with images of her legs wrapped around me, those beautiful eyes filled with passion.

She tilts her head, considering my words. Then her lips curve into a smile, slow and sultry. "I don't belong to anybody, Chadwick," she says.

"You belong to me. There's no debating that."

She regards me while she drinks, and the wolf inside me feels like it's beating me to death. It wants her. *I* want her. I don't know how much longer I can . . .

She takes me by the hand and slides off the barstool. "Let's go to your place. I don't think you're allowed in my dorm."

She leads me toward the door, and I follow, doing my best to hold myself together.

Alpha's One-Night Stand is now available on Amazon!

Free book from Ariel Renner

Want more paranormal romance & fantasy romance from Ariel Renner? **Get a free novella** when you sign up for her email newsletter!

Scan the QR code above or go to:
arielrenner.com/pb-free-book

About the Author

Ariel Renner became enchanted by Disney fairy tales at an early age. Anime, Marvel comic books, and love songs on the radio further fueled her fascination with magical worlds, superhuman abilities, and happily ever afters.

She published her debut novel, *Forbidden Ice Prince*, in March 2023. Ariel loves crafting spellbinding tales of enemies-to-lovers, destiny, strong heroines, fiercely protective heroes, epic battles of good versus evil, and true love. Through her books, she hopes to offer a unique twist for fans of paranormal and fantasy romance.

Ariel lives in Frisco, Texas with her husband and their beloved corgis. When she's not writing, she enjoys traveling, binge-watching crime dramas, and filling her home with pop culture collectibles.

Discover more of her books at: **arielrenner.com/books**